My education was se(
highly thought of by m
through the system and seemed to come out the
other side with a reasonable education.

I went to the West of England College of Art and
studied Commercial designing. I did this for several
years but found I was not getting enough from it, to
satisfy myself.

I became interested in the printing process, and
went on to become a press operator. I moved up
the chain and ended up as works manager.

When the business closed, I took exams to sell
insurance with the Cooperative Insurance Society,
until I retired.

I often told stories to my grandchildren, and
when I was asked to write one down, I thought,
Why not? The result is this book.

I now have six books, and I am writing the
seventh.

I am 77 years of age.

Other Books Written by the Author:

Children's books
Ten Quests
Ten Kingdoms
Ten Elements
Grandad's Extraordinary Camper Van

Adult books
Those Among Us
Those Among Us Return

Dedication

I dedicate this book to my wife, Jennifer, who has supported me at all times as I created this book. And to Theo Roberts, my grandson, who was the first young reader to read my story. His comment, *When is the next story of Scott going to be written,* inspired me to go on writing.

John Parsons

TEN QUESTS

To William

Hope you enjoy the

book

AUSTIN MACAULEY PUBLISHERS™

LONDON • CAMBRIDGE • NEW YORK • SHARJAH

A CIP catalogue record for this title is available from the British Library.

ISBN 9781788483353 (Paperback)
ISBN 9781788483360 (Hardback)
ISBN 9781788483377 (E-Book)

www.austinmacauley.com

First Published (2018)
Austin Macauley Publishers Ltd™
25 Canada Square
Canary Wharf
London
E14 5LQ

Acknowledgements

My thanks to Jennifer and Anne Knight, who read my book at its early stages.
To my grandchildren, who wrote down ideas that might be used in the rooms Scott encounters.

Chapter 1
A Door Opens

Scott had passed the old house many times as he went to school, but had never been in the garden or walked up the path to the front door. Not that he had any reason to do that. Everyone had stories about the house; some said it was haunted, some said it was a witch's house and others said people who went through the front door never came out because they were eaten alive by 'Trolls'—whatever they were.

No, Scott had no desire to find out. The house was a three-storey building on one side of the entrance. A half circle castle-like turret was on the other side with a spire and a bat weather vane on its top. Spooky or what!

It had a window on the third floor, and on the second floor was a collection of windows going around the house suggesting lots of rooms.

At the front of the house was the porch, and this lead to the front door. Any person who wished to come out from the door could watch anyone coming along the drive as they approached the house. Three steps up from the drive brought the visitor to the front door.

Other windows could be seen to the side of the house including the turret that had windows in it, one above the other. The roof was dull blue grey tiles that suggested it may be local roof tiles from the quarry down the road.

Scott usually cycled past, hardly giving the house a glance. He was coming up to his fourteenth birthday and had been playing football with his friends on the local field where he had been training for the village youth club team, 'Smithfield Lions'.

He wasn't a great player but he really enjoyed his game, and as a winger, had created many goals with his swift and accurate passes to the centre for the strikers to finish with a goal.

'Smithfield Lions' were second from the top, and promotion beckoned.

It was said that when a challenge came about, Scott was the one to work out some sort of a solution. He had a quick mind and a strong body—his friends often said it was a killer combination.

Not that Scott was a bully, it was because he did a lot of sport, and so his body had toughened up and left him slightly taller than his mates for his age.

Oscar, Jack, Finlay and Kyle cycled back with Scott from training. They all played for 'Smithfield Lions' and were all good friends.

It was, as they followed the bend in the road that would take them past the gate to the house, that a movement by the entrance caught their eye. The gates to the drive were open and were swinging in the wind.

There had always been a chain on the gates to stop people entering, although in truth, it would not take much effort for anyone to climb over the brick wall surrounding the property, but who would want to?

The lads skidded to a stop and looked down the drive. They could see the porch area of the house quite clearly and the front door was also open.

"What's going on do you reckon?" said Scott.

"Bet some old geezer's bought the house," said Jack.

"Nah," said Finlay, "it's the Troll; he's hungry and wants to eat another kid."

"Shut up!" said Oscar, who was now looking very scared.

Finlay grinned at Oscar and looked at the others, "Oscar's messing his pants. He's so scared."

Kyle looked at Finlay and then at the rest, "None of us are feeling sure about this, if we are honest," he said, "it's spooky after all this time and now, well, it looks sort of 'normal', if you see what I mean."

Jack, who had always been the most daring one of the group, stood on his pedals, and with a cry to the others of "come on, let's find out what's going on," raced on down the drive towards the front door.

"He's gone mad," said Oscar as he watched Jack pedalling down the drive still calling out 'come on' to the others.

They watched Jack arrive at the steps that led up to the front door and then held their breath as Jack dropped his bike on the edge of the steps and looked back at the others.

He looked into the open doorway from the bottom of the steps and then moved sideways to get a better view.

"He's still alive," said Oscar with a hint of amazement in his voice.

"He's a nut case," said Kyle.

"Well, here goes. Are you coming lads?" said Scott as he stood on the pedals and started down the drive towards the steps in front of the house.

"Another madman," said Oscar, "I'm going home before the witch's spell gets me," and with that, he stood on his bike pedals and cycled on down the road, keeping his eyes away from the house in case the spell caught him.

Finlay and Kyle watched him disappear around the bend and then looked at each other.

"My mum nags me if I'm late for dinner," said Kyle, hoping that Finlay might take the hint to go.

"Mine goes on and on about my homework," he said.

With a grin to each other, they looked one last time at the two friends at the steps of the weird house.

"Jack, Scott, we are going home as we have homework to do and our dinner's ready," they called out, and they stood on the pedals of the bikes and were on their way.

"They are scared," said Jack. "Who in their right minds would rush home to do homework?"

"Well, I'm not exactly excited that we are stuck outside a haunted house," said Scott.

"Come on," said Jack, "let's go up the steps and get a closer look."

"If someone's moving in, what do we say if someone comes? We shouldn't be here doing nothing, they might think we are stealing or something."

"Oh Scotty, don't tell me you are scared also. We can say something like 'can we get you something from the shops, like some milk or bread' if they come," said Jack.

"Okay, but anything spooky and I am gone from here."

The two boys slowly ascended the steps until they were by the opened door.

As they looked in, they could see a staircase coming down from a second story with a parapet going around the floor above for anyone to look down into the hall. Doors could be seen leading from both upstairs and downstairs, all in line with each other, one above each other.

"Cor," muttered Jack, "look at that."

"Bit posh, isn't it?" said Scott.

The balustrade ended with a carving of two dwarf like figures on the end and Jack noticed that one was on the top of the stairs but not on the other side.

"Do you think someone nicked the other one at the top of the stairs," said Jack?

"Don't know," said Scott, "but it looks odd with two downstairs and only one upstairs."

"No one around," said Jack, "should we call out, do you think?"

"Let's just go," said Scott, "we have had a look and no one's noticed us. They would be here if they had."

"I wonder what's behind the door," said Jack. "There could be a suit of armour."

Before Scott could stop him, Jack stepped inside the house and walked around the door for a look.

"Nope," he called out, "just a picture of the outside of the house."

Scott stayed outside but was worried about Jack; he was inside someone's home and shouldn't be there.

"Jack," he called, "come out now, we are going to be in big trouble if you don't."

"This is weird," said Jack from behind the door. "I am looking at a picture, but it's moving. It's not a window it's definitely a painted picture, but people, as they pass the gates, are moving. Look, there goes a car!"

"Just a quick look then," said Scott as he stepped inside and turned around the door.

Sure enough, it was a painted picture but it was moving, even the leaves on the trees were moving in the picture. He could see his bike and Jack's on the path, and the steps leading up to the door.

Jack moved around the door and called out to Scott as he passed out onto the balcony, and down the steps to the bikes, "Am I in the painting now Scott?"

Scott looked in amazement as he saw Jack jumping up and down in the painting.

And then it happened!

Chapter 2
All Is Not What It Seems

The door slammed shut with a loud bang that seemed to vibrate throughout the house.

Scott ran to the door to open it and get out, his heart beating fast as he reached towards the handle.

But there was no door handle!

How could this be? He glanced behind him to see if anyone was coming but no sound could be heard.

He ran his fingers over the door in a frantic effort to open the door. Nothing! No secret press-switch, no keyhole—nothing. He was locked in.

He remembered the picture, perhaps it was a window, and maybe he could get out through that, if it was.

He was getting desperate as he turned to the picture next to the door. He could see Jack outside calling out but could not hear him.

He felt along the picture trying to find a latch that would open the picture if it was a window, but alas, it proved fruitless. It was a picture, weird, but a picture. *My mobile phone. I can ring my Mum and Dad, and they can get me out of here*, he thought. He searched his trouser pockets but found nothing. His phone wasn't there. Nothing was in his pockets.

Panic started to affect him, his breathing increased and he needed to sit down. He was almost in tears as he sat on the stairs; waiting for what, he had no idea.

It was at this point that he decided to try one of the doors—if he could go into another room, he might be able to get out another way.

His mind made up and his nerves a little more steady, he got up and moved towards one of the doors.

As he reached a door, he paused, looked around and then reached out to take hold of the door handle.

"I wouldn't do that," a voice said behind him, making him jump as he withdrew his hand, as if his hand had been burnt.

He slowly turned around expecting to see the house owner—but no.

In front of him was a boy about the same age as him, another on the bottom of the stairs, climbing down from the balustrade and, as he looked around, a third boy was coming down from the top of the stairs.

They were dressed in weird clothes, each like the other, wearing a tight trouser suit with wood grain patterns running up or down it.

As Scott looked down, he saw that the shoes also had the same pattern on them.

"I'm sorry I'm in your house uninvited, I didn't want to come in. I'm not a thief, please, I just want to go home," his words just poured out without a breath.

"It's not our house," said the second boy, the house belongs to no one other than those in it. You could say you own it now and it owns you!"

"Not yours, mine! I don't get it, what do you mean by 'it owns me'?"

"I think you need to sit down and we will explain what happened to us and then you can start your quest."

"Quest? You have lost me. Who are you if you don't live here?"

"Well," said the one on the stairs, "we don't technically live here—we just exist here. Look around you. What has changed since that first boy came in and you then followed?"

Scott looked around. "The doors shut," he said.

"No, no," said the boy on the stairs, look again, think about what you saw when you looked in, and what is not there now."

Scott looked around again. The painting was the same with Jack kicking the door then running down the steps in case he got into trouble. He looked at the doors on the ground floor then looked up at the balustrade.

"The carvings are gone," he said, "there were three, two at the bottom and one at the—" His voice went quiet as he looked at the three boys.

"Top!" chorused the three boys.

"Yes, we are the three you saw."

"No, no, I must be dreaming," said Scott loudly. "This cannot be happening."

"I'm afraid it's true," said one of the boys. "You have become trapped in this house and your being here has brought us back to life."

"Well if that's so," said Scott, "let's just open the door or smash a window and get out of here."

"It's impossible," came the reply.

"I don't understand why you don't just leave, and how can you be the carvings I saw on the ends of the stairs? This is stupid. I can't believe I am hearing this. I must be dreaming and I will wake up soon," and he then pinched himself and winched as he felt the pain.

"I am not dreaming," he said almost in tears. "Can't you open the door for me to go home, what's happening to me?"

"Sit down and we will tell you," the third boy said at the top of the stairs.

Scott, with shoulders slumped, moved to the stairs. He was feeling very sorry for himself, his mind buzzing with questions but no answers. What was going to happen to him? How could he get home if these boys really were magic boys who could change into carvings on the end of the banisters?

Wait till he got outside with Jack, he would beat his mate to pulp, tear his hair from his head, rip his ears off, break every bone in his body and if that wasn't enough, he would think of more. Then he almost started to cry as he realised that he might not ever get out of this weird house.

"Now we are going to tell you what happened to us and how we became part of this house. Sit on the stairs and listen."

"Okay," said Scott, "but after that, I am going to look for something to smash a window and get out of here, you are not keeping me in here."

Scott sat on the stairs and the boys gathered around him.

"I am the first," said the boy who was nearest to Scott and who had spoken first.

"I'm the second," said the boy on the bottom of the stairs, "and at the top of the stairs is the third boy who was the last to join us."

"I know it's a lot to take in at the moment, but if you could just take a deep breath and clear your mind of all of the questions you are asking yourself and listen to us, we may be able to give you some answers."

Scott looked at the first boy and, with a deep sigh, asked, "Do you all have names?"

"Oh yes, we must have when we came into the house," said the first boy, "but we don't use them now. We found that even our names are forgotten, it seems the house erased our memories of our home, our mother and father, so as we are here forever, we just call ourselves One, Two and Three."

"Forever?" said Scott. "What do you mean forever?"

"Well, we failed to do the quest," said Two.

"The quest?" asked Scott.

"Look, let's start at the beginning," said One, "then you won't be asking questions at each point."

"This house has some sort of spell on it, it's not haunted but it is magical. You noticed the picture when you came in. This is the very thing that caught us. When you looked out, you saw the trees moving in the picture, your friend jumping up and down. It's not normal is it?"

"No, it's blooming weird," said Scott.

"It's more than that," said Two.

One looked at Two and said, "I will tell him," and turned to Scott.

"This house either has a curse on it or it's magic."

"The strange thing is that it opens its door now and then and a new boy becomes trapped. It's like a fly trap, once it's got what it wants it shuts the door and then, and only then, we come back to life."

"Oh no, no, no," muttered Scott, "this can't be happening."

"I'm afraid it is," said the boy called One.

"But why me?" asked Scott.

"We think that it selects the boy that it thinks might be the best person to beat it on the quest. As you looked out of the picture, it was looking at you."

Scott was on the point of crying again. *This can't be true,* he thought, *Jack would rush home and tell his dad and he would come and get me.*

As his mind rushed through these thoughts, he felt himself calm back down.

He looked at the three boys—they seemed normal enough.

He reached over to One and softly pinched his arm. Yes, he was flesh and blood.

"We are real now," One said, as if he had read Scott's mind, "but if you fail the quest, then you will become one of us."

"One of you?" asked Scott. "Do you mean I'll live forever in here?" he asked, almost in tears again as the thought of never seeing his mum and dad hit home.

One looked at Two and Three, and then turned to Scott. "The answer to that question is yes, but it is up to you. The house has lots of tests for you to go through before it will let you go. We all failed the quest and we have been here ever since. We have no idea of time; there is no clock in this hall, no beds, no kitchen and no food. We just don't seem to need any. We can't remember when we last slept, ate or even went to the toilet! Things are not normal in this house."

Scott looked at One and said, "You don't wee or poo? You are having a laugh, everyone does that!"

"Not once the house closes the door. Then you become part of the house. You don't feel thirsty, do you? But it's been a long time since you last had a drink I am sure."

Scott thought for a moment and realised that he wasn't thirsty or hungry, yet he had been on his way home for his meal.

"Once you go through a door, the quest starts," continued One. "We can't help you on the quest, but we can tell you that you have got to get to the other door at the other side of the room that you have entered."

"So this is why you told me not to open the door," said Scott. "But how hard can it be to enter a room and go to the other side and into the next room."

"The hard bit is getting across the room," said Three. "I was the last one to try and I got seven rooms conquered before I failed. Just three more and I would have been out of here instead of being a carving when the door opens for the next person to enter—that being you."

"So are you saying that if I don't do this test, that if I fail in some way, I become a piece of wood like you," Scott said?

"Not the best way to put it," said One, "but basically, you are right. We may have been in here for years and years. We just don't know. Once we failed, it seemed but a moment before the next one of us came in through the door. All I remember was seeing a new boy come in through the open door and look around. I couldn't move but I could see."

"Once he looked at the picture, the door closed," went on One.

"It was then that I became aware that I could move, and I climbed down from the balustrade. I had no idea how I got there but when I spoke to Two, he jumped and very nearly fainted. I explained to him, just as I am to you, what had happened to me and then, after a cry and an angry period, he kicked the doors, tore up the picture, jumped on it and then decided he had no other choice but to try to do the quest."

"But the picture is still there," said Scott.

"Yes, you will need to get used to that—the house puts everything back to as it was," said Three.

"He really tried on the quest but as he will tell you, he didn't get far."

Scott looked at Two who shrugged his shoulders and said, "I didn't think things through. You have got to work out your moves first before you start. When you go through a door, you will find a long red stone. Once you step from the red stone, the rooms quest starts."

"I was in an ice room and fell into the water, the next thing I know is I am watching a new boy come in through the door that turned out to be Three."

"An ice room?" asked Scott.

"The rooms are not like any normal room with tables and chairs, each room is different. You can step into a jungle, or into a room that's an island in a huge lake and you will then need to swim from one island to another that has the door on it for you to exit back to here."

"This is just madness," said Scott. "How can a room be a jungle or a lake?"

"You will see once you start through one of the doors."

"We are trying to prepare you for each room, because each room is another world," said Two.

Scott turned and looked up at Three.

"As I said before, I did seven rooms but it is not enough. The house wants ten."

Scott scratched his hair in puzzlement then stood up and faced the three boys who sat or stood on the stairs. "How do you know that the house wants ten rooms conquered?" he asked.

"Come with me," said One and stepped down the few stairs, and walked around the hallway and under the stairs.

There on the wall was what looked like ancient writing and as Scott looked, the writing changed to English.

Scott looked at One, then back at the writing.

He read:

You that have ventured into my domain
Will never leave this house again,
Save but for one chance, I give
Fail and forever in this house you live.
Ten rooms await to test your mind
One route from each room you will find.
Should you go wrong, from a path you stray
Then in this house you'll forever stay.
Succeed on ten, and then no more
Your success for all, will open the door.
Beware then stranger, twill be your skill
That ends your quest and breaks my will.

Scott looked at One and then moved back from under the stairs.

"It says on the wall that it will open the door for all. It could mean that you and Two and Three could also leave if I succeed."

One looked Scott in the eye, put his hands on his shoulders and said, "We think so also, but we must rely on you, as we failed totally.

"No room is the same. Rooms that we have been in never seem to appear exactly the same again. All I can say is, you do need to take your time before you step from the red stone. Each room you come out of changes colour from the brown you see on each now.

"We assume that this indicates that it is done. You will not be able to redo the same one having solved it. Three managed to change the colour of seven doors and then entered the eighth door.

"We don't remember anything more until now when we saw your friend and then you come through the door. The house didn't want your friend, if it did, it would have closed before you came in. You were cautious, thinking—not impetuous like the first boy. The house must think you will give it a challenge. So do we."

One dropped his hands to his side from Scott's shoulders and turned and sat down. He knew it was a lot to take in. How can a house have a mind of its own? He watched Scott standing there, a puzzled expression on his face.

If only he was the one to break this curse, he thought.

Scott wandered over to the stairs and sat down.

He looked around him at the doors, they seemed to be arranged in a circle of ten around the stairs that were coming down to the ground floor.

His eyes looked at the arrangement of doors upstairs as he lifted his head to take the balcony doors in.

Again, ten doors to choose from, and a small staircase in a spiral wound up to a single door on a third floor. He looked at the boys, who were quiet, watching his reactions.

Scott stood up and walked upstairs, and walked around the balcony looking at the ten doors—no door gave any clue to what was inside the room.

He started up the spiral staircase but found the door at the top had a lot of bars and locks on it.

"What's going on here?" he called out.

"We don't know, but it's not a room that is part of the quest," called out Two.

He came back down and looked at the front door again, then looked at the ten doors downstairs.

No handle had miraculously appeared on the front door—he had no choice.

He looked at the picture and saw Jack lifting his hand and waving as he shouted at the door, but he could hear nothing.

He turned to the boys and said, "When do I start this quest?"

"Whenever you want," said One.

Scott took a great breath and turned to the boys. "Which one do I start with?" he asked.

"It doesn't matter," said One. "The rooms will all be different, so try any one. Just one more thing, please remember that once you step from the red stone, the quest in that room has begun. Go in and step sideways, or as the door closes you may be pushed from the red stone before you are ready."

Scott looked at the other two boys and then turned to the nearest door.

He felt a little sick, just as he did before a football match. 'Nerves', his trainer and coach called it.

He reached for the handle of the door and pressed the bar down, then as he heard the click of the door opening, he pushed the door open.

"Good luck," called all three boys as he took a step in. Then, as he came to the edge of the door, it pushed Scott as it tried to close, almost knocking him over. He had forgotten the warning given to him about not looking around before going into the room entirely.

BANG!

Chapter 3
The First Quest Begins

The door slammed shut, knocking into Scott and he almost fell from the red stone he was on. He turned and looked at the door. There was no way back from this side; no handle was showing on this side of the door. He had to move forward.

He looked around the room, but this time, taking his time.

The colours were weird. He was in another world, that was for sure.

It seemed, at first glance, to be a woodland path in front of him. The view was vast and not a room in the true sense of its meaning.

He stood on the red stone and took a good look around. The ground lifted up from where he stood but he could see the path in front cutting through the hills on either side of its course.

The sky was green! The path was blue and, as he watched, a white cloud followed the contours of the land, dropped down to the path then up over the hill on the other side.

It was as if it was all upside down.

It was!

Scott realised that he was watching an upside down effect.

If he stepped from the stone onto the path, would he fall through it? Should he stand on the clouds?

All sorts of thoughts raced through his mind.

He reasoned that if the blue of the sky was the same as the grass he would normally be walking on, then he should walk on the blue in front of him and avoid the white clouds as they came.

The red stone beneath his feet shuddered and grew smaller.

"What's going on?" shouted Scott who had almost fallen from the stone. He looked down and found that the red stone had shrunk to half its size.

"I guess you want me to start," he said aloud, then realised that he was talking to himself. Did he really believe that the house was watching him in this room?

Room—that was a laugh, he thought.

He stepped from the stone onto the blue path and was relieved to find that he was on a solid footing. He had this part right.

Scott started following the pathway, keeping an eye on the clouds moving towards him.

As he walked, he noticed that the bushes on the hillside were also upside down. What he had assumed were bushes with no leaves on them—like in autumn time—were now the roots of the bushes, and the leaves and small stems were, in fact, the tops of the shrubs—but on the ground. This gave the illusion of low scrub growth at the base of the plant.

Then, as Scott looked more into what he was seeing, he burst out laughing.

Daffodils were upside down in big clusters—the yellow trumpets on the ground with a long green stalk and big leaves at the top, crowned by a bulb, with roots blowing in the wind.

This is a crazy world, thought Scott as he restarted on his way.

Scott noticed a big cloud making its way towards him and he decided to run to try and miss the cloud, in case it was a danger to him.

It had not affected the trees as it passed but he was not part of this crazy world, so he was taking no chances.

He had almost made it when a small bit of the cloud passed under his foot. He began to sink!

"I knew it," shouted Scott as the cloud drifted by.

Scott fell forward as his feet sank into the ground just like in a bog.

He grabbed hold of a bush in front of him and pulled himself towards firmer ground.

Scott lifted his knee up onto the edge and, still using the bush, pulled himself up and out of the blue bog that, as he watched, became firm ground again while the cloud drifted away and blue sky slowly showed.

If I was still in that, I would have been trapped as it dried, thought Scott.

He followed the path, keeping an eye on the sky around him in case another cloud came near him. It was strange how he had, in such a short time, become quite used to the sky being on the ground— and the need to walk on it!

As he came to a bend, he noticed a lot of trees—all upside down—growing along and up the side of the banks.

This must have been an avenue of trees once, thought Scott.

He walked below the overhanging roots and again noticed the branches on the ground, with dense leaves on the ends of the branches where they were on the ground.

Although he was below the overhang of the tree roots, sky still showed on the ground and Scott suddenly realised that another cloud was approaching.

He ran up to a tree and climbed up the bough and up onto a part of the tree. He was now not on the ground.

The house had no rules and so the tree started to sink onto its side with Scott slowly moving towards the ground.

He swung around to the other side and the tree started to tip to that side.

Scott looked around quickly as the tree sunk ever closer to the cloud-covered ground.

He swung around to the original side he had been on and ran along the bough.

When he was close enough to the next tree, he reached out, grabbed that tree's branch and swung onto its bough.

He climbed higher through the branches and looked for another tree touching the tree he was on.

As the second tree started to sink into the ground, he jumped to the next tree and circled this one to get to the other side.

Moving along the branch, he looked down and saw that the cloud had gone, it was firm blue showing once again.

He climbed down and looked at the damage he had caused to the trees he had climbed on. The first one was now just a trunk and roots, sticking above ground; the second had part of its branches with leaves buried in the ground and small branches sticking up above the ground.

"Sorry trees," he said aloud, for he felt badly about the chaos he had caused among the trees.

Scott continued around the bend and then, as the path became straight again, slowed down as he took in his next unusual sight.

In front of him, Scott could see between the upside down trees that the path led to an upside down house!

As he walked nearer, the house slowly came into full view.

Yes, it really was an upside down house.

The roof was the base of the house, and it looked as if the chimneys, if it had any, had sunk into the ground.

Scott moved closer, looking at the house and wondering how, whoever lived in there, entered the house. He started to walk around the house but as he went to the side, he bumped into an invisible wall. He could see through the wall but could not go around it. The upside down house just continued as if the invisible wall was not there.

He turned and walked back to the front then past the edge to try to go around the other side, as again, he could see around the side of the house. This time he held his hands out in front of him and soon made contact with the invisible wall again.

He felt the wall and found that went to the floor. Satisfied that he could not go under, he thought he would try to go over. He looked at the trees nearby.

Moving to one that he felt would be near enough, he climbed up the tree and once he was level with the base of the house, he moved along the bough that would have been close to the ground if it was upright.

He was near the end of the bough when he hit the clear wall again.

He returned along the bough and climbed up to the top where the roots of the tree fanned out. He was at the highest point now.

Again, he walked towards the invisible wall, along the root, balancing as it became thinner. Soon, he came to where he judged the wall would be.

Again, he touched the wall and reached up to see if it had a lip that he could hold on to and pull himself over—no such luck.

He reversed his way back, then climbed back down to the blue floor.

Looking at the house again he reasoned that, as he could not go around it, he would have to go through it, but how?

As he studied the upside-down house, his eyes moved slowly up the building. As his eyes reached the front door, it slowly opened inward and a hand popped out and beckoned him up.

Scot looked around, then moved backwards to see if he could see the owner of the hand. As he got a better view into the doorway, so the hand retreated into the house until it was lost from view.

"How do I get up there," shouted Scott.

Nothing happened.

"Can you throw down a rope, please?" shouted Scott.

Again, nothing happened.

This is stupid, thought Scott, then shouted up to whoever was inside the doorway, "I'm only a schoolboy. I didn't ask to do this stupid quest."

The house must have disliked Scott's last comment—it was its game after all.

A large, black, storm cloud gathered very quickly and moved toward Scott.

As it approached, so rain fell upward from it towards the green sky.

Scott watched as the rain rose upward and then ran to the house.

Rain splashed upward against him and ran up his legs, soaking his body. He was soon so wet that the rain was dripping from his head upward to the green sky.

Scott hung on to a ledge of the house that was part of the overhang to the house roof, as a precaution against sinking into the blue ground.

He was safe, it would seem, as the house did not move when the rain poured upwards. Perhaps black clouds were not one that he could sink in to.

The black cloud moved on and soon the blue ground returned.

Scott looked up and again he saw the hand beckoning him up, so taking a deep breath, he started to climb up towards the first window.

He found that he could use the rough stones on the house to hold on to and to stand on as he moved upward.

As an extra help, he had started his climb near the drain pipe so that he could use it if he needed to.

At last, he made it to the window and tried to look in, but all he could see was a reflection of himself.

This is a really weird place, thought Scott and bent his elbow ready to smash the glass. But before he did it, he looked up and the hand was beckoning him, once again, to climb to the door.

"Oh hell," cussed Scott, for he didn't want to climb up to the door, but he started to climb up to the next set of windows.

Once he got to them, he stopped and looked up at the bottom set of windows and the door.

He had passed the single window of the three-storey house, reached the mid-section and now had the last bit to do; to get to the door.

He started once again, taking care as he was aware that he was now quite high up and did not want to fall.

As he moved up, he came to the top of the doorway and gripping the edge, pulled up as his legs pushed him higher.

His body was now almost halfway past the doorway, but he could see no one there.

He heaved himself up and bending forward, crawled into the passageway. "Hello," he called out.

Scott slowly stood and looked along the passageway. It was as if the house had turned itself the right way up but only on the inside, as far as he could see. Light bulbs hung down from the ceiling, carpet on the floor—it was so weird that Scott had to check if the house had done a reversal on the outside once he had climbed up and into the door.

No, he thought, *still upside down on the outside*, as he looked down to the ground.

It was then that he became aware that he was no longer soaking wet. "This is a crazy world I am in," he said aloud. "I guess the house didn't want my wet shoes on the carpet!"

He turned again to look along the corridor and saw a hand waving to him, beckoning him to come to it.

"Look—whoever you are," called out Scott "are you going to show me the way out from this house?"

No answer came and Scott moved on down the corridor looking behind him every so often, as he got nearer to the doorway where the hand continued to beckon.

Just as he neared the doorway, the hand withdrew and Scott hastened to the entrance to look in.

This was a kitchen, quite normal, not upside down and quite a spacious area, one that his mother kept saying she would like, he thought.

He entered the kitchen and looked behind the door. No one was there. The owner of the hand was nowhere to be seen.

The kitchen was oblong in shape with a centre island. He had seen the like in magazines that his parents purchased—the sort that the rich and famous were photographed in.

He moved around the kitchen and completed the circle around the room.

As he got to the door, he noticed a piece of paper on the floor. *That wasn't there before*, he thought. He picked it up and read it.

PLEASE SHUT THE DOOR AFTER YOU ENTER.

Why would anyone print out a message like this when they could just ask me? he thought.

Looking out of the door along the passage again and seeing no one, he stepped back into the kitchen and shut the door.

The handle disappeared in front of him and a continuation of units grew from each side and before he could do or say anything, the door was gone and the kitchen units were a full circle around him.

Scott stepped back and tried to calm his breathing down, he was in a state of fear, shock and amazement. He had just witnessed magic, hadn't he?

Once he calmed down, he started to look around again. No evidence of any doorways out. No windows either. How was he to get out?

He moved back to the kitchen units that had 'built' themselves in front of the door.

First, he opened the lower doors but they were all empty—other than shelves, no part of the door could be seen. It had a very solid back to it and although Scott pushed very hard, no movement occurred.

He moved around the kitchen opening doors but after quite a while, all the cupboards proved to be just that—cupboards!

Scott stood on the counter in front of the top cupboards but they also proved to be empty, and door-less.

He climbed back down and leaned against the centre island. He had checked them, nothing unusual at all. There must be a way out.

As he looked around him with a slight rising of panic, his eyes settled on the cooker and the oven.

It couldn't be, could it? he thought.

Scott rushed over to the cooker and dropped the cooker door down to expose the oven. It was a passageway! As he looked into the cooker, he could see a hand in the distance, beckoning him once again.

Ducking down, he put his head inside and then his shoulders. He didn't touch the sides. It was as if it was expanding, as if to accept his body.

Scott reached forward and drew the rest of his body inside and soon he was lying inside the oven.

He began to crawl forward and, in very little time, his head came out of the passageway from the oven into another room.

The owner of the hand was nowhere to be seen.

"I'm getting used to your disappearing act," he said loudly for, in truth, he was a little annoyed. He hadn't asked to do this but what could he do about it?

He climbed out from the oven passageway and stood looking around.

He was in a library. Lots of books—all on shelves built on walls—but again, no door or window. He turned to look at the oven exit but it had gone, books on shelves had replaced it.

On the far side of the room was a ladder to climb up to reach the top shelves and the books.

He had seen a secret doorway in a film on TV when watching it with his Mother and Father, and it had opened when the hero had pulled a book from a shelf.

Moving to the books, he started trying to pull the books out—but they didn't move. He could grip them but they stayed where they were. He continued around the room, but all to no avail.

He looked at the ladder.

'This must be here for a purpose,' he thought, *'as it's not for getting books down.'*

He climbed up, and taking hold of a book at the top, pulled it. Nothing, it was just like the others.

He reached out and pulled several more and just as he was about to give up, the book he took hold of dropped forward, and there was a click as a panel of books opened on the other side.

Scott climbed down quickly and looked through the small doorway.

Yet again the hand beckoned him.

Scott crouched down and half-ducked, half-walked along the passageway.

He couldn't look up as he went along this route as he was squatting down as he went. He came to a set of steps.

It was now possible to stand and Scott eased his back as he rose and looked up. Again, the hand beckoned him.

"This really isn't funny," shouted Scott. "Why can't you wait for me and let me see you?"

The hand disappeared from the top of the stairs and Scott ran up, determined to see this time, where the owner went to.

He entered a lounge slightly out of breath as he entered through a doorway, but no one was in the room.

He had been right behind the hand's owner—but nothing.

What if it's just a hand, he thought, *some ghostly form leading me through the strange house.*

He had a cold shiver run down his back as he thought this.

Well, if it is, he thought, *it's doing okay so far, and no harm has happened to me.*

He glanced behind him but no doorway was evident; the house had put a wall joining the rest, and he had not noticed.

He looked around the lounge and noticed that it had windows at both ends. The lounge had a settee, two lounge chairs, a fire place with a pile of logs to one side, a set of little tables and, as you would expect, a TV.

A tall unit with music discs stacked along one shelf and a disc player on it was to one side. A reading lamp stood behind one of the chairs and a newspaper was lying over one of the armrests.

Pictures on the walls of futuristic scenes completed the room.

Scott moved to the window and looked out. He was looking at the upside down land he had walked through. He could see the blue ground with clouds moving across it, and the green sky—nothing had changed.

He turned and walked to the other end of the lounge. Against the wall were tall dressers that contained glasses and little statues of creatures, the like he had never seen before.

One was what looked like an ogre—a big bulky figure with a big red wart on his nose.

Is it a wart? thought Scott.

He slid the glass door open and reached in to grasp the figure in order to look more closely, but as his hand neared the figure, the head moved and the mouth opened on it.

"Wow," said Scott as he withdrew his hand and shut the glass door quickly.

"That looked as if it was going to bite me," he said aloud. "This really is a crazy house with ornaments that can come to life."

The figure had resumed its original stance and Scott had no wish to try again. He moved to the other window and looked out.

This was a 'normal' view with grass on the ground and sky above as it should be. He was looking at the back of the house, the way he assumed was the way to the end of this room's quest.

Could he open the window was his next thought.

Scott examined the window quickly and found that no opening windows were available to use.

This was a blow to his plans, as he felt that if he could get out, he could climb down the house and reach the ground.

Could he break the window?

He looked around for something that he could lift and throw at it to break it. *Not the ogre statue*, he thought.

He moved back to the stack of little tables and thought that one of those would be great to smash the window.

Scott looked around as he reached for the little table, for he was feeling guilty about his proposed act of vandalism.

He stooped down and tried to lift the little table but it didn't move.

Scott tugged, pulled and heaved but to no avail, the table stayed put.

I guess that's no good then, thought Scott, and moved around the room. He reached one of the pictures and tried to lift it down, but it was as if it was glued to the wall—it just didn't move!

Time for a rethink.

Scott now knew that he must continue his journey through the house and not try to do it from the outside.

He went back to the dresser with the ogre statue and opened the lower doors. Inside were boxes of toys—weird spaceships and spacemen in one, a train set with a track to run the engines on in another.

Nothing was behind the boxes that he had removed.

He turned and moved back to the settee and arm chairs. He lifted the cushions out but no door was available. He could see the floor through the springs.

As he stood up, he glanced towards the dresser he had emptied and was amazed to see that the boxes he had left on the carpet had disappeared.

He made his way back up to it and again opened the lower doors.

Everything was back where it was before he took it out.

"Wow, my mum would like some of this magic in my bedroom," said Scott aloud, "she's always moaning about how untidy I am."

He turned to go back to the settee and chairs and saw that the cushions he had dropped on the floor had also been replaced.

"I keep saying it, but this is one crazy house," muttered Scott as he continued to think about getting out of the room.

He moved to the fireplace and looked at the logs. The fire grate to burn the logs was in the middle of the fireplace and as Scott moved nearer, he had an idea. The chimney!

He moved into the fireplace and looked up.

A set of iron steps hung just above his head and he reached up and pulled them down. It was not unlike the ladder to the loft at home—as he pulled it down, so the sections locked into place.

This must be the way out, thought Scott and started to climb.

As he disappeared from the room, so he could see light above his head and yet again the hand beckoning him up.

Scott continued up the ladder until he came to the passageway that the hand had been signalling to him from.

Above him, he could see that the chimney was blocked, so he climbed into the passageway and crawled along it. Again, it wasn't dark—although Scott had no idea where the light was coming from.

He could see the end and the hand doing its usual job of encouraging him along.

Scott reached the end and crawled into the next room.

He was in a bedroom.

In front of him was a four-poster bed with drapes folded back on each corner. He had seen this sort of thing on visits to big houses that his parents took him to. The drapes would draw around the bed to keep the cold out in winter-time, as the old houses had no central heating that they have in modern houses.

This thought caused Scott to feel a little sad again, as he recalled the comments said by the strange wooden boys.

He mustn't think of them like that, they were just boys now and he hoped he could finish this quest and get out.

"Well, I am not going to fail and become a trophy on the stairs," he said aloud and, taking a deep breath, he crawled into the room and stood up.

Pictures, once again, were on the wall but the room had no windows.

As he swivelled around, he saw that the hole he had come into the room by, was gone. It was just part of the wall now.

At the bottom of the bed was a huge trunk and he lifted the lid and looked in.

Lots of old-fashioned clothes were folded and stacked inside it.

Scott reached in and lifted some out and dropped them on to the floor, then returned to emptying the box.

After totally removing the clothes, he stepped into the box and felt all the way around for any latch that would open a secret door.

Nothing. He jumped up and down, but nothing happed.

Stepping out, he moved to the side of the bed and opened the little cupboard by its side. He pulled out the drawers and stooped to look through. No passageway presented itself to him.

He stood and moved back to the box at the base of the bed. The clothes were gone!

He opened the box and looked in. The old dresses and shirts were all back just as they were when he had first opened the box, all neat and tidy.

"I've got to get a pinch of this magic," said Scott aloud.

Not a lot of items were in this room and Scott had to find the way out.

He climbed onto the bed. Should he have taken his shoes off?

They were clean, or sort of—the mud had dried and did not seem to be showing.

What am I worrying about, he thought, *'it's a magic house and it will clean up after me,* and he walked across the bed to the drapes hanging on one of the posts of the bed.

They were tied back, revealing the room. He examined the headboard at the back but no latch hidden there opened a doorway.

He untied the drapes and when they were hanging down he gripped it and wrapped his legs around it like a big fat rope and climbed up to the bed's roof—not an easy task—but he made it.

He looked over the top but apart from a pile of dust, no doorway was there.

He slid down and sat on the bed.

It was quite comfortable and he thought how in the 'old days' they would sleep in this bed.

Under the bed. The thought rushed into his mind and he leapt from the bed and onto the floor.

He lifted the coverings hanging over the side of the bed and looked under.

He couldn't even get his head under it, but could just about get his arm under. That wasn't the answer.

He climbed onto the bed and rested his back against the back of the bed. He needed new inspiration to come now.

Could he shift the mattress, he wondered. He got down again and got to the corner of the bed.

Throwing the covers from the overhang, he took hold of the mattress and tried to lift it. Nothing happened. He tried pulling it. All to no avail— nothing moved.

He climbed onto the bed and sat once again looking into the room.

He was getting a little fed up now, he felt that he had done quite well so far, but this room was beating him.

While he was puzzling about it, a thought that had nothing to do with his problem came to mind.

It was quite simple; he wondered what it would be like to have the curtain drapes drawn around him, and what would it feel like?

To hell with it, thought Scott, *why not?*

He moved to the bottom of the bed and untied the sash that held the bottom drapes and, once released, he drew them across the bottom.

Next, he undid the other one and drew that to meet the other one. He returned to the head of the bed and undid the sash there and drew the curtain to meet at the bottom of the bed.

Lastly, he returned to the one he had used to climb up and drew that to the bottom of the bed. He was now enclosed on the bed. As he crawled

looked under the table but no door. As he stood back up, he was amazed to find that the pots and pans had been reassembled and were all stacked just as before. He had not heard a thing.

Scott looked around again and could not find any other place to look.

It must be something on the wall, he thought.

He started to move around the walls pressing any funny mark in case it was a button or feeling for a small latch that would open a door.

He finally came to the boiler end and the toilet. He squeezed between the boiler and the wall and again came to the toilet.

Scott again went inside and felt along the walls but found nothing.

He came out and touched the boiler by accident as he had been careful not to touch it in case he burnt himself.

It wasn't hot.

He moved to the front and bent to look in at the viewing hole that he could see the red flames flickering through.

Strange, he thought, as he put his hand out towards the face of the boiler, *no heat at all and yet it appears to be on and burning.*

He looked at the big wheel on the front of the boiler and then thought about the gloves.

Returning to the table, he picked up the gloves and drew them on.

He reached out and started to turn the wheel to unlock the boiler door.

The door unlocked and swung away from Scott to reveal a passage going into the boiler and steps leading down. He looked at the inside of the door and saw an imitation fire behind the glass inspection panel that he had seen from the outside.

Scott took off the gloves and threw them down, then stepped into the big boiler. It wasn't hot, it had been an illusion that the boiler was on. He hadn't even needed the gloves!

He walked in and started going down the steps.

At the bottom was a corridor walkway and he followed it until he came to a stop in front of a full-sized mirror. It was as if the mirror was a door but no handle was available to open it. He could just see a perfect reflection of himself.

He looked around but could see no latch on the side of the frame.

He wondered if he had to swivel it. Taking both frame edges, he pushed on one side and pulled on the other. No movement occurred.

Just as he went to step back and before he let go of the frame, he noticed a shimmering effect on the glass. He let go of one side of the frame and touched the glass. It was solid.

Yet he was sure it had changed when he was touching both sides.

He reached out and touched both sides but did not hold the frame and sure enough the glass changed to the shimmering he had seen. He pushed his thumb to the glass and watched as it went through the glass.

He withdrew his hand and looked at his thumb. Nothing wrong with it. He wriggled it and bent it but it worked as normal—but it had gone through the mirror.

What to do now was the question.

He had to pass through the mirror, of that he was certain, but how could he maintain the touching of both sides until he was through as he could become part of the mirror if he broke contact.

After a little thought, he came up with a sort of plan. He would step through backwards keeping his hands touching the edges of the mirror frame by letting his fingers just slide along the edge as he stepped through.

Taking a big breath and with his heart beating very fast, he backed up to the mirror.

Pressing his back to the mirror, he reached out and touched both sides of the frame and felt the solid mirror behind him disappear.

Holding as steady as he could he lifted one foot and moved it backward over the bottom part of the frame. He looked down and saw that his foot from just below the knee was gone—it had gone through the mirror.

Putting his weight on his foot that was inside the mirror, he pushed back and saw that his lower body was now in the mirror.

He was now bending, keeping his hands touching the mirror frame.

He gripped the frame and lifted and pushed his other leg through. Now he was half in and half out.

He let go of the frame but making sure he kept touching the frame and stood upright and slid his hand again, but inward towards the glass. He took a slight step back and his head and the top of his body came through the mirror.

Now only his hands were part way through. Making sure he was always touching the sides of the mirror, he withdrew them and, once they were through, he released the frame.

The mirror reverted to a mirror.

"Phew," said Scott, "that was really spooky, not to mention scary."

He turned and looked at the room he was in.

It was a large room with a dining table running down the middle of the room. Chairs were pushed up to the table as if waiting for people to come to take their places to eat.

The table was set out with knives and forks, spoons and large mats in the middle, ready for the meal to be served. Napkins in little rings to the side and wine glasses at each placement completed the layout.

Scot looked behind him but this time, the tall mirror was still there.

He turned and started to walk around the table looking at it and any hangings on his way. A large woven cloth hung against the wall, covering part of the surface. Scott held it away from the wall to see if it hid any way out.

Nothing showed that looked unusual, so he let it drop back into place. Next he came to a set of pictures on the wall and looked at them, not as a painting but as a possible doorway. Anything was a possibility in this house.

He took hold of a big painting and held it away from the wall it was hanging against, this was not easy as the painting was heavy.

He repeated this with all the paintings and dropped the last one against the wall as it again proved to be fruitless in his quest for the hidden doorway.

He continued around the room until he again came to the mirror he had come into the room by.

He now turned his attention to the huge table. He walked around it again, looking for some clue that might suggest what he should do.

A message or a note, maybe a menu card. Nothing.

He bent and looked under the table. Nothing obvious there.

He was at the head of the table resting his hands on the back of the rather posh chairs when he noticed a bell next to the salt and pepper mill on the table.

Why was that there?

He picked it up and rang the bell.

Behind him and to the side a panel had opened in the wall and a serving hatch had appeared.

Scott moved over and looked at the hole. A box shape was showing inside and he remembered that, in one of the old houses he had visited with his parents, a serving hatch like this had been shown to them. It was called a dumb waiter.

He climbed inside and rang the bell. He started to descend and held on to the sides as it moved down.

After a short journey, it came to an end and he got out, stepping into another corridor.

He followed it along and as he went towards a bend, he saw once again the hand beckoning to him.

Without thinking, he rushed forward after the hand and unfortunately tripped over something.

It proved to be a mat and he landed on it on his stomach. His momentum caused the mat and him to slide along the passageway and, before he could stop it, his route along the passage started sloping down.

As the forward momentum pushed it forward, the downward slope increased and still lying headfirst on the mat, Scott started sliding down a chute that twisted and turned through the walls of the house.

There was no way to stop it—he just clung on to a piece of rope that seemed to be attached to the mat.

Finally, the chute straightened out and as he looked up, he saw he was hurtling towards a door with a large square metal frame in it.

Before he could do anything—as if he could have done anything—there was a loud clang and Scott shot through the square frame as he and the mat hit it, and the metal frame on a hinge lifted for him and the mat to go through.

He had just gone through a giant cat flap!

As he and the mat slowed in a cloud of dust and came to a halt, Scott realised that he was through the house and on the other side.

He slowly got up and looked around. The house behind him that he had just left was the right way up. He had no idea how that could be, but the sky was blue above him, trees were standing tall with roots in the ground, as one would expect and grass grew alongside the dusty pathway he was on.

It was normal.

He turned his back on the house and started to walk along the path towards the bend that he could see.

As he rounded the corner, he saw in front of him, a door standing upright with no visible support around it, and a red stone in front of the door.

Scott moved swiftly to it and stood on the red stone. He reached for the handle and pressed it down.

It opened and Scott stepped back into the hallway where the three boys were. He had come out from the door that he had entered through in the beginning.

Behind him, the door closed and Scott turned to see that the door had no door-handle now and, as he watched, blue paint ran upwards from the bottom and green ran down it from the top. The door was painting itself.

"Crazy, isn't it?" said One.

"Well done, you completed that one and came back to us safely," said Two.

"Do I always come back through the same door that I had entered through?" asked Scott. "Oh yes, every time. But don't ask me how, as I have no idea," answered One.

Scott looked at the green and blue door that now had half painted with the sky above and grass below and the other half in the reverse order. The boys asked what the room was like and Scott told them of the green sky and how he had almost lost when the cloud had passed over him on the blue land.

He told them how the house cleared up after his mess and how the hand beckoned him.

"Are you ready to try another one then, Scott?"

Scott turned his back on the painted door and walked across to the opposite side and stood in front of the door that was directly opposite it.

"This one then, I think."

Chapter 4
The Second Quest

Scott took hold of the door handle and noticed, as he pressed down on it, that it was shaped like a tiger jumping. The door opened and he quickly stepped in and to the side, so that the door couldn't push him from the red stone.

Scott looked in amazement as his eyes beheld a jungle with a small dry mud path leading away from the door and the red stone.

As he watched, he saw a troop of monkeys swing from one side of the jungle across the path to the other side.

"Awesome," he said aloud. He was just going to step down from the red stone when he saw some yellow eyes looking at him from the long grass at the base of a tree in front of him. As he looked, he could make out the shape of a tiger.

As he watched the yellow eyes, he became aware of movement on the other side of the path—and so did the yellow eyes!

A small deer could just be seen in the tall grass on the other side. It seemed unaware that the tiger, or indeed Scott, was watching it.

Scott almost called out to the deer to warn it but then stopped. If the tiger got its dinner, then it wouldn't want Scott! It was cruel, but as Miss Smith, his teacher, said: 'It was the law of the jungle.'

He held his breath as the deer moved closer to the tiger, still on the other side of the path hidden in the long grass.

Suddenly, the tiger sprang from hiding and bounded across the path. The deer, at the sound of the tiger's snarl as it came from the grass, turned and ran deeper into the jungle and was lost to the sight of Scott in moments. The tiger disappeared just a moment after it.

Without thinking, Scott stepped from the red stone and ran to where the tiger had disappeared.

He could hear the snarling and roaring of the tiger in the distance and he hoped the little deer got away.

He looked back to look at the door—the door was gone and so was the red stone!

He quickly turned his back to where the door had been, and started to run through the jungle, brushing away vines and big leaves that were in the way of the progress following the path.

He was getting hot and could still hear the tiger in the distance, and the path was now getting smaller, as the jungle closed in on him.

He barely had time to notice the colours of the flowers or the butterflies around him; his mind was set on getting out by finding the door.

Swinging his arms to the left and right, he was able to move the hanging vines to allow his progress. It wasn't easy as he had to duck down very low on a few occasions.

Monkeys chattered above his head and on one big vine, a green snake wound its way up towards the top of the tree.

A fallen tree blocked his way, and Scott had to climb over it to continue on the pathway.

Scott could hear water running ahead of him, and he ducked under another vine covered with leaves, but as he stood, he almost fell into the water.

Across the water, he could see the door and the path leading up to it.

How do I cross the river? he thought.

He looked around; on both sides of the path that he stood on, there were thick prickly shrubs, trees hung over the path with the usual vines hanging down. No chance of pushing through this.

The answer must be the trees, but how?

The answer came as he heard a roar behind him from the still-hungry tiger.

Monkeys ran up the trees, swung on vines across the river and disappeared.

Scott reached up for a vine that was swinging towards him from the other side of the river that the monkeys had used to escape. As he grabbed hold of the vine, he pulled back and reaching as high as he could, swung with the returning vine across the river.

Alarmingly, the vine started to lower Scott towards the water as he came towards the middle. He was going to hit the water!

He quickly thrust his legs forward and his body backward, just as he did on a swing, and with the extra momentum, he zipped past the water and started upward.

As he reached the other side, he let go of the vine and dropped to the path.

Scott heard a roar behind him and saw the tiger on the bank on the other side.

That was a close thing, he thought, as his heartbeat slowed back down.

Just as he was beginning to relax, the tiger jumped into the water and began swimming across.

Scott turned and ran as fast as he could towards the door, which seemed to be a lot further away than the last time he looked.

Monkeys screamed at Scott and the tiger, as it reached the bank and climbed out of the water.

Still running, Scott glanced behind him and found the tiger was now running after him.

He could almost feel the tiger's breath on him as he jumped onto the red stone.

He reached for the handle of the door and pulled the door open. As he went through, he glanced back, but no tiger could be seen.

He realised that once on the red stone, he was safe, just as he was at the start.

The door slammed shut and then started to run with green paint.

"This house is really weird," said Scott, as he bent over, trying to get his breath back.

He glanced back and noticed that brown was now falling down the door but not showing on all of the door.

"A really crazy house, and it's trying to kill me!" said Scott. He had forgotten that tigers were not afraid of water!

As the three boys came up to him and patted him on his back saying congratulations and well done, Scott watched the door he had come through turn into a camouflaged-patterned door.

"Oh you went to a jungle room," said Two.

"Yes," said Scott, "I got chased by a tiger."

"I think mine was a lion, but it may have been the tiger," said Two. "I don't remember how I got on, so I guess I got eaten."

"One thing I have noticed about this quest," said Scott "is to stay on the red stone and look around before stepping down; I almost didn't and just noticed the tiger's eyes watching me before I stepped down."

"Good job you noticed it then," said Three, "or you would be waking up as number four at the top of the stairs."

Scott looked at him and suddenly felt a little sick, "That's the last thing I want. Sorry, guys!"

"Are you ready for the next door?" asked One.

"I think so," said Scott. "Fingers crossed, lads."

Scott looked around, then went upstairs. He picked the door directly above the first door he had gone in, now painted with the two halves of sky and ground on it.

"I'm going to give this one a try," he said and reached for the handle.

Chapter 5
The Third Quest

Scott pushed the handle down and stepped into the room, then stepped to the side as the door slammed shut.

He turned and looked at the door, the lack of a handle again was evident.

He turned back to look at the room.

It appeared to be another long narrow room but filled with water, but not just water.

What looked like a log was just by the red stone he was standing on—and it had eyes!

The water was muddy brown; he couldn't see the bottom, but he could see that there was an awful lot of logs! Crocodile logs!

What was he to do now?

He studied the sides of the room, and noticed small climbing notches on the left side and then halfway along, there were none. He looked across to the other side and noticed that halfway along on the right hand side, the small notches continued. There was none from the red stone on the right side.

On looking at the notches, he became convinced that they were like the hand and foot notches he had used on the climbing wall in the school grounds. He, like all of his friends, got on quite well on this, although it did require a lot of concentration and body strength. It was a good job that Scott was a burly lad; his football training for stamina and his past experience of wall climbing would be of help on this challenge.

Scott followed with his eyes the way to the end of the left hand side, looking for the highest route he could find. He didn't want to be the meal for the 'logs'!

"How do I get to the end," he said out loud to himself.

"There must be a way I can get over to the right hand side to go on using the hand notches that start over there."

He looked again and again. Nothing. It looked as if he was going to have to take a chance and drop into the water, and swim or wade across and get out before the crocodiles caught him. Impossible! If he didn't find the solution, he was lost.

He had spent a long time studying the layout and suddenly, the red stone partly withdrew under the door leaving him with just a half to stand on.

"I guess the house is getting impatient with me," he said aloud. As the red stone had withdrawn, so the crocodiles had lifted their heads in anticipation of a meal.

Scott decided to do his best without a solution as to how he would cross over to the other side, once the climbing notches ran out on this side.

He reached from the red stone, and took hold of a handhold then stepped onto the first notch below it. He had planned on the visual mapping done before, to guide his best and safest route.

He glanced below and saw the crocodiles following him along. One opened and then snapped shut its jaws. Scott squeezed his handhold a little tighter, they may be hungry, but he was determined he wasn't going to be dinner.

Scott made slow but steady progress along the left-hand side-wall and was getting close to the part where the notches ran out when it happened.

As he reached across for his next handhold, his foot slipped. He lost his grip with the foothold and he was now hanging by one hand. The crocodiles were getting excited as their next meal hung close to them.

Blood dripped from Scott's scraped knuckle into the water and this excited them even more.

One took a leaping surge up, using another's back to reach high and just missed Scott's foot.

Scott swung his hand across, grabbed the hold he had been going for and then lifted his feet, one after the other, to bring him back to a safer position. He stayed there for a while, resting his aching arm before he continued. His knuckle hurt and still bled.

After a few moments, he started to move again, and at last came to the end of the hand notches.

What now?

He looked over at the other side, to the notches and followed them by eye to the door. Yes, this was the way to go—but how?

He became aware of a piece of very fine nylon cord above his head and, climbing higher, got level with it.

It stretched across to the other side but would not be strong enough to use to swing across as he had in the tiger room.

He took hold of it, making sure this time that his foot and handholds were firm.

He gave it a pull towards him to see how strong it was and heard a *click* as he pulled and then released it.

His mouth opened in amazement as a clear heavy plank moved out from the wall opposite but stopped half way. He couldn't reach it!

Should he swing and jump?

He thought about what he had done and then took the nylon cord again but this time pulled it from his side. Again, the *click* and a second clear heavy plank came out from the left side and met the right hand side one.

He now had a bridge—if it was safe!

Scott climbed a little higher, then eased himself onto the clear plank.

Catching hold of the sides, he pulled himself along the plank as this was the only way to cross with very little room above his head.

At last he was at the join and he reached ahead to pull onto the right hand side section. He was almost fully on when it started to withdraw back into the wall.

"No, no," yelled Scott, but he hung on tightly as it drew him closer to the right hand wall.

With no time to think about it, Scott readied himself to grab a handhold as it neared, if he missed, then he was dinner.

As if they knew what was going on, the crocodiles were getting in a frenzy below him.

He had chosen the notch he felt looked the best and leaned over a little more to enable him to grab it in a strong hold as it came nearer.

His body started to slip down as the plank disappeared and he was soon just hanging on the end as it eased into the wall.

With one really strong swing, Scott grabbed the notch he wanted and hung with one hand as the last bit of the plank disappeared.

His arms were aching now but he swung up, grabbed a second handhold and in a few moments had added support for his feet.

After a short rest, and wanting to get out of that room, he started taking a route away from the crocodiles, towards the door.

This time, without any more problems, he made it to the red stone and stepped down.

He reached for the door handle and saw that it was a crocodile handle. Slightly out of breath, Scott opened the door, passed through and the three boys rushed over to greet him.

The door behind him slammed shut and he turned to watch it paint itself.

This time it was a dark green, but once it finished, it became knobbly, just like a crocodiles skin, but no handle.

"Weirder and weirder," said Scott.

"We are all glad you completed that one," said One.

"It took a long time and I almost didn't make it on two occasions," said Scott.

"It doesn't seem like a long time to us," said Two. "You see, you seem to go in through a door and then it opens again and out you come."

"But I was in there for ages," said Scott, "and very exhausted doing it; my arms were aching, I was bleeding and I was very tired," said Scott.

"And how do you feel now?" asked Three.

"Well, now that you are asking, I am not aching and, well, I guess I feel about the same as I did before I started," said Scott.

"That's the thing about this quest", said Three, "if you beat the room, it puts you back as you were before you entered the room. I suppose it's what is called giving you an even chance. I did the most and after each room, once I came out, I was strangely back to my original self; not tired, no cuts, no bruises."

"Did you scrape or cut your hand or foot at all," asked Two?

"Yes," said Scott and looked at his knuckles on his hand. Much to his surprise, nothing showed—his hand was just as if he had not scraped it when he had grabbed the wall notches as he fell.

"I almost lost a leg to a crocodile in there," said Scott. "Are you saying that if it bit my leg off, I would be back to normal once I hopped out of the door?"

"I guess I am, but I just don't know. Remember, I got eaten I think, so there was no way back for me."

Scott looked at the three boys and said "Are you sure I have got to do this to get out?"

"It's the only way I'm afraid," said One.

Scott walked over to the front door and saw that no handle was available to open it.

He moved to the picture and was amazed to see Jack was still outside calling his name, although he couldn't hear him.

Why hasn't he called my mum and dad, thought Scott.

He then turned and asked the same question to the boys.

"Because time has no meaning with the house, remember what we told you a moment ago. You go in through the door and come straight out again. Time is yours and the rest of us are as if nothing is happening," said One.

"Okay. The sooner I get this quest done, the sooner I can go home," said Scott, and turned and marched across the landing to the door above the second one downstairs that he had done.

"Let's see what this one will give me."

"Good luck," called the boys as Scott raised his hand to the door handle.

Chapter 6
The Fourth Quest

He gripped the handle and pressed down. The door swung open and he stepped in, remembering to step away from the door as it closed on its own.

In front of him was a deep, deep valley with high rocks on both sides. He could see the door on the other side but how was he to cross?

I wonder if it is a valley or just appears so, thought Scott.

He picked up a loose stone on the red stone and threw it to the middle of the valley. If it was a mirage and not real, then it should bounce on the floor.

He watched as the stone went on down and down, and finally disappeared. *Well,* thought Scott, *this weird house has done it again, it's a sheer drop if I don't make it across.*

Looking to each side of the door, he saw planks leaning against the side. They were about eight inches wide and as he tried lifting one, found it to be surprisingly light, but they were also clear, just like glass.

How can I use these? he thought. Would they be strong enough so that he could use them? *They are too short to reach the door yet. They must be there for me to use as an answer to the puzzle.*

He looked at the mountain-side and noticed that there was a V shape sticking out at regular intervals along the mountain-side and this occurred on both sides.

I wonder if I can push a plank from the platform to one of those V spikes, thought Scott.

He drew in his mind a zigzag pattern with each plank resting on one of the Vs, then the next from the middle of the first plank to the opposite V. How many planks did he have? He would need twelve, he estimated. He counted the planks and found he had thirteen. An unlucky number, maybe the house was thinking so.

He stepped down from the red stone to begin the quest.

He found the nearest V shape to where he was standing and taking a plank, lifted it and lowered it towards the V on the side. He made contact with the V on one end and lowered the end he was holding. It rested on the platform so he pushed it a little more onto the V.

So far, so good.

Now he needed to get the next plank on to the V on the opposite side.

This was the scary bit. It would mean stepping on to the first plank, walking so far out over the void with a plank in his hand and place the next plank on the V on the opposite side and then rest the other end of the plank on to the first plank, thus creating a zigzag walkway.

The problem was that he had to trust the V supports, and get over being able to see through the glass-like planks.

He turned to the stacked planks and took the next one.

He thought he could crawl out holding the plank but as he started, he realised that he would have to stand, balance as he walked holding the plank, and step to roughly half way to then get the next plank into position.

He hated to look down but had to as he balanced the plank. He stepped onto the first plank and slowly walked out, trying not to think about the great deep void below him.

He made slow progress and at last reached the half-way point.

Lowering the plank, he turned it so that it was pointing to the V on the other side. Slowly, he lowered the end to the V and made contact with it. He lowered the end he was holding to the plank he was standing on and breathed out with a big sigh. He must have been holding his breath as he had been positioning the plank.

He turned and walked back to the stack of planks.

Ten more to go, he thought.

Taking his next plank, he started his way out onto the first plank, then on to the second until he was at the angle he needed to locate the next plank on the V, again on the opposite side to maintain the zigzag. Again taking his time, he located the plank on the V and lowered the plank to the plank he was standing on.

He was gaining confidence as he did each one and slowly worked his way across the void.

He was becoming a little too sure of his ability to finish this room and the house must have been aware. The house had plans for Scott to lose!

It happened as he was taking the tenth plank across the void. As he got into the position to place the plank that he had carefully carried across, a loud crack above him caused him to look up to see what it was. Lots of stones and two big boulders broke away from the side and fell towards Scott. Before he could do anything the first big boulder passed by his side just missing him and the plank path.

Scott ducked down and rested the plank he was carrying onto the plank he was on, and held the rest over his head.

Please don't break the planks I have done, he prayed, as small and some quite large stones fell on the planks around him and on the one he was holding.

The second big boulder passed by without hitting the zigzags or sweeping Scott from the plank.

Then a quite large stone struck Scott's hand holding the plank and he let the plank go with a cry of 'Ouch!' The plank tipped up, wobbled for a moment on the plank Scott was on, then followed the stones and boulders into the deep void.

More stones and dust continued to fall but eventually stopped and the dust disappeared.

Scott looked at his hand bleeding from quite a bad cut, then felt his head at the side where a stone had struck him once the plank was lost.

He withdrew his hand and found that it was bleeding, he was also bleeding in his face, just above the ear.

"You don't play fair," he shouted angrily.

There was a tremor from the house and small stones started to fall from the sides, and the planks began to sway.

Scott fell to his knees and held onto the plank.

The tremors stopped and slowly he stood up.

He turned and made his way back to the other side to collect a replacement plank, aware that he had just enough now to complete the task. His head hurting, still bleeding and his hand still sore from the stone striking him, he picked up another plank and made his way across the divide to place the plank into the next sequence.

With a struggle he located the end of the plank, rested the end onto the plank he was standing on and turned and walked back to the next plank.

He continued carrying the planks one at a time with a lot more difficulty than before the rock shower. Scott was very purposeful in his endeavours to finish the job, and as he worked, he tried to forget the pain he was in.

Finally, he came to the last one and started on his way.

He got to the end and was just manoeuvring the plank onto the platform when the house played its last trick.

A loud crack sounded and boulders fell from above the platform and door he had come in by.

Scott was unaware that he had turned to watch but was horrified to see a huge boulder sweep away two of the planks. The planks started to collapse into the void, for nothing was now supporting them.

Scott turned and ran along the last plank and jumped just as the last plank dropped into the void.

He jumped onto the red stone but the house had not finished with Scott. It was angry with him. Stones continued to fall and two hit him on his shoulder and his head, almost making him fall from the red stone.

Scott grabbed the door handle, pushed down and opened it just as another stone hit his back.

He passed through, and fell to his knees.

Blood was falling from his head and his hands were bleeding. Pools formed as he looked down.

The three boys came across and helped him up.

"We thought that you were beaten when the house shook," said One.

"I very nearly was," Scott said as he looked back at his hands. As he watched, the cuts healed, the cuts stopped bleeding on his hands and down his head, and the weakness disappeared.

"I am never going to get used to this," said Scott. "The house tried very hard to kill me, caused me great pain during the challenge, and then repairs me only to try again to kill me." Even the blood on the floor had gone.

"I know it makes no sense," said Three, "but it must do to the house. It's as if it is playing with us, showing us that it can do what it wants. The problem is—we don't know what it wants!"

"What happened in your room to cause the house to shake?" asked Two.

"I think that was me," said Scott. "I told it that it did not play fair and it got angry."

"Oh dear," said One. "Try to remember next time that the house has control over you and you have no control over it. Try to focus on finishing the room's challenge as easily as you can; the house can, as you found out, make it harder for you."

"We know it's in our interest that you finish all of the rooms; we know you can do it," said Three.

Scott thought for a moment and then said, "You are right, I must not lose sight of the goal. My trainer in our football club often tells us this."

"What is football?" asked One and Two.

"Don't worry answering that now," said Three. "They must have come into the house a long time ago."

"Well I guess the house is ready for my next attempt so I think I will go downstairs and try another one from there."

So saying, Scott ran down the stairs leaving the three boys leaning over the banisters.

"Which one now?" said Scott and moved towards another door.

Chapter 7
The Fifth Quest

Scott picked the first door after the front door, on the side away from the painting. He did not want to see if Jack was still outside. He doubted that he was, as he had been inside the house for what seemed like hours now.

He pressed the door handle down and tried to open the door. It wouldn't open. He tried again but this time he pulled and was pleased to find that it opened easily. He stepped inside and eased the door shut, the house was not going to push him by reversing the opening of the door. He was in a square room, more like inside a cube he thought. He looked around but no exit door could be found.

Scott looked down to check if he was on the safe red stone, but there was none—he had already started the challenge.

So, he thought, *the house is punishing me for shouting at it.*

He turned around to look at the door through which he had come in, but to his amazement, there were nine cubes set in the door frame. The whole door was just like a giant nine square puzzle.

He stepped back and the cube he was in tipped back, causing the nine cubes forming the door to fall to the ground. Now he did have a puzzle!

Scott picked up one of the door pieces and looked at it. It was a part of the lower panel of the door, a dark dull-green colour. He turned it over and found it was a top of the door, but a slightly different lighter dull green.

Looking around, Scott could see that every part of the cube he was in had a frame like the one that held the door he had entered through.

"I guess I must make the door up with the nine pieces and then open the door," he said.

He moved with the piece to the opposite side, to the frame of the door he had come in on, but, as he did so, the cube tipped further towards the frame.

Pieces slid towards him and Scott got on hands and knees to get to the frame piece he wanted.

At least the pieces came to me, he thought.

He chose the slightly different lighter dull-green piece as he thought the exit door must be a different colour. *I can only try it*, he thought. He was making the door up almost on the floor.

He placed the piece into the frame where he thought it went, then, still on hands and knees, picked a second piece.

Slowly, he made up the puzzle and as the last part went in, the nine parts merged into one and a handle appeared.

"Well, that was quite easy," he said, but only to himself—he was well aware the house listened, and would punish him if he wasn't careful.

He moved back a little and, as the cube moved back, watched the door he had made change to a real door. Now it didn't break or fall. At last he was almost upright, and pressed the handle down and pulled. Nothing! *Stupid me*, thought Scott and pressed the handle again and pushed. The door swung open and as Scott took a step forward, the cube tipped forward, causing him to go through into space! Scott was hanging onto the handle and around him, were stars and the blackness of open space.

As he struggled, so the cube rocked.

He reached around the door and put one hand on one handle outside and left his other on the inside.

He was now facing back into the cube as he hung by the handles. He started to swing his legs back and forth, causing the cube to rock and roll. His arms were aching but if he let go, the game was over and he would become the latest carving for the house.

Gaining momentum, he flicked his legs into the doorway and pulled himself up. The cube rolled sideways as his legs made contact and Scott pushed himself further into the cube, as the door swung. He let go of the handle on the outside and pushed even more against the remaining handle with his other hand.

He was almost in now, so he let go of the handle as it swung upward and dropped towards the floor grabbing the edge of the frame and pushed the rest of himself into the cube, letting go, as the door tilted towards his fingers.

As the weight over-balanced the cube, the door he had just built, and fallen through, slammed shut, and broke into nine pieces.

Scott lay on the floor. His heart was beating very fast and he was quite exhausted.

He had almost lost because, once again, he had assumed that things were easy. Nothing was easy in this house!

The only thing I can say about this is: I must have picked the right colour door to make up the exit, thought Scott. *Well there's no reason to think about the near failure; I must make up the next frame, but how can I keep track of which ones I have done?*

Scott looked back at the door he had done, then back to the opposite space where he had come in.

If I do the other two to the side, then it will leave me with the ceiling and the floor, he thought.

Not wishing to cause the cube to move too fast and making sure it didn't tumble, he eased his way over to one of the side walls that was one he needed to do.

Again, the pieces followed him as he stood and leaned into the panel.

Picking up a piece that looked like the lower part of the same coloured door he had selected, he placed it to the base of the frame. Moving the pieces, he found the next part he wanted and slotted it in. Finding the last piece of the base of the door, he made up the first part of the door puzzle.

Next came the middle section.

He picked up the middle piece, put that in then the hinge part against the frame. He picked up the handle piece and placed that in. *It's not that the making of the door puzzle is difficult,* thought Scott, *it's what could be behind the door.*

He slotted the rest of the three pieces into place and stepped back slowly as the door in front again became a door with the handle available to press to open.

Scott walked forward and pressed the handle down and pushed the door open letting it go on its own, hanging on to the side frame of the door.

Rocks and stones passed the door and some hit the red stone outside the door and bounced inside, hitting Scott.

It was the chasm with the deep void below that he had done with the planks.

A large stone hit him and he fell backwards, and as he did, the door swung shut and as before, broke into nine pieces.

Resting for a moment he then turned to the opposite side and slowly standing, placed his hand in the centre of the panel and again started to rebuild the door in a new frame.

If this isn't it, thought Scott, *then I only have the ceiling and floor to do.*

He almost completed the door when he became aware of the blood running down his head.

"Oh no, not again," he said loudly.

The stone that had struck him had caused him to have a cut to the side of his head.

He pushed the last piece into place and prepared himself for the opening of the door.

He watched as the door became a real door and then moved to it and pressed the handle down.

He pushed it open.

Snow blew into the cube and it was so heavy that Scott could hardly see out of the door.

Just then he heard a roar and made out the shape of a huge polar bear running towards him.

He quickly backed away and the door swung shut as his weight caused the cube to rock back just as the bear jumped towards the opening.

Again, the door turned into nine pieces and fell at his feet.

"Goodness me that was close," said Scott out loud, heart beating fast with the shock.

Scott eased into the middle of the cube. The floor was covered with stones and snow, the room was now very cold, but his wounded head had stopped bleeding.

This leaves the ceiling and the floor, he thought.

Scott looked down to the floor and then picked up the first piece of door puzzle and moving slowly, placed the first piece in the bottom corner. He had done this puzzle three times now and knew the way it fitted.

He had to step away from the door he was making to allow the snow and stones to fall from the area he was working on.

At last he had just one piece to place in, to complete the door puzzle.

Placing the last piece in, he stepped back to cause the cube to become upright. He watched as the door changed and moved slowly forward to open the door. *This must be the one,* he thought.

As he took hold of the handle, he noticed it was shaped like the jumping tiger handle.

"I will open it," he said aloud, "in case the house is spoofing me and wants me to not open it thinking it's the jungle room."

He slowly pressed the handle down and pushed it open.

Sure enough, it was the jungle room and monkeys scampered across the path in front of the door.

He stepped backward and in so doing, caused the cube to tilt away from the door. The jungle door swung and slammed shut. Pieces fell to the floor and Scott turned to the last place to build the door—it was the ceiling.

The ceiling was now in front of him, opposite the jungle door position.

He picked up the bottom door piece and began building for, what he hoped, would be the last time. He soon had the bottom pieces in and started the second row.

The cube started to rock!

"Oh no, please let me finish this last puzzle," he shouted aloud.

The rocking slowed and stopped.

"Thank you," said Scott, and returned to the placing of the pieces to the door puzzle.

At last, he had the door made up and moved slowly towards the door.

As he watched, the door puzzle became a door, and he reached for the handle. He pressed it down and pushed it open.

"Yes," he said. He stepped back into the hallway and was greeted by the boys.

"What happened," asked One. "The whole house shook and we thought you had failed."

"I was on the last part of the puzzle and the cube started to shake, I think the house was still annoyed with me, and so wanted to stop me completing the quest through the door."

"Puzzle? Cube? Whatever have you had to do?" Asked Two.

Scott moved over to the stairs and told them all about the cube, how the door became the puzzle taking him to some of the places he had been in some rooms prior. He told them of his first encounter with the cube door and how he had almost fallen into space.

The boys sat looking up at Scott with mouths open, listening to his telling of each door. When he came to the snow door, Two said, "I went there."

Finally, he told of the final door in the ceiling and how, as he built it, the cube had rocked, almost causing the pieces to fall.

He told how he had called out to the house to please let him complete the puzzle and the shaking had stopped.

"That must have been when we felt the vibration in the house," said One.

"I got some nasty cuts, one on my head from the stones that were falling behind one door," said Scott.

"Well, they aren't there now," said Three.

"It's so strange the way I feel exhausted while I am doing the challenge but now it feels, well—" he paused, thinking, then said, "normal; if anything can be normal."

"Well, five done and five to go," said One.

"I am going upstairs and going to do one from those," said Scott.

As he stood, he looked at the three boys sitting on the floor at the base of the stairs where they had been listening to his story of the cube just done.

He looked at the door he had come through and smiled. The door had changed colour to show squares of nine blocks on the outside, each block a different colour.

He turned and walked upstairs to the landing and advanced to the door directly in front of him.

"This one will do, I think," he said in a low voice and taking a deep breath, grasped the handle and pressed it down. Without looking back at the boys who had followed him up the stairs, he opened the door.

Chapter 8
The Sixth Quest

Scott stepped in and looked down as he stepped sideways.

The red stone was back in this room.

He looked up and around the room. In front of him were hands floating up and down or side to side, palms up. Nothing seemed to be controlling them, they appeared to be attached to nothing. Some were small, some large and at the far end of the room was a door with a red hand, palm facing up, on it.

Now what do I have to do here? thought Scott.

He studied each hand as it lifted and fell, then the ones moving side to side.

"I cannot think what I need to do in this room," said Scott aloud to himself.

He looked at the door across the room and then again at the hands floating in front of him.

"I guess I need to jump from one to another and make my way to the door," he said again aloud.

He watched the routine of the hands and decided it was time to go.

He stepped from the red stone and walked to the edge, and timing his jump as the first hand moving sideways came near him, he jumped onto it. *So far so good,* he thought.

As he stood there on the hand, he watched for a hand to come near that was going up and down; he needed this one as it was the only way he could make his way across.

As the hand came near him and the hand he was stood on drew nearer, he readied himself for the jump.

Timing it just right, he jumped slightly down to the rising hand and landed just right. As he rose, he looked for the next hand he needed and saw one quite away from him.

The hand he was on was moving quite quickly and the one he wanted was very slow.

I am going to have to wait, he thought.

His hand reached the top of its lift and began to drop.

As it descended, Scott watched the next hand moving slowly towards him from the side.

"It's going to be close but I should make it," said Scott.

The hand he stood on reached its lowest level and started to rise again.

Scott kept his eyes on the oncoming hand and as he was raised up on the hand he stood on, the hand he wanted next drew closer. It wasn't going to be easy after all, as the slow hand was still quite away from him. As the hand he stood on drew up to its highest level, Scott waited, then took his chance, as he saw the slow hand move just below him. He dropped onto it as it slowly passed below the hand he had been standing on. He almost stood up, but remembered to stay down as he passed under the hand he had jumped from.

The house has placed the hands just right to knock me from them, should I forget, he thought.

He glanced below the hand and could see nothing. Just black nothing.

I don't want to go there, he said to himself.

Now he was on a slow hand moving side to side. He needed a hand moving up and down to progress further.

He had worked it out that to enable him to reach the door with the palm sticking out, he would need to get on one hand going side to side then one going up and down, then repeat one side to side and then up and down until he reached his target.

He had ten hands to navigate to reach the door.

He watched for his next target hand, one that was going up and down.

He found the one he wanted and positioned himself at the finger's edge—ready.

Slowly, the hand moved towards the next hand he wanted. It had dropped to its lowest point and was on its way back up.

The slow hand wasn't going to get close enough to the next one that had now gone up above the hand he stood on.

Will it come down in time? thought Scott.

The hand reached its height and started down, and was soon level with the hand Scott was on.

Scott watched as it went on down and very slowly, the hand Scott was on reached the area that the other hand had dropped to.

Scott moved back from the fingers to the back of the hand and looked down. Below him was the hand he wanted, still going down.

Without thinking, Scott dropped from the palm of the hand he was on, onto the hand below.

He hit the middle of the hand and dropped down on his bottom. He had done it.

He waited for the hand he was on, to come back up and as it rose, he looked for his next hand to help his journey.

It was crossing just in front of him, so he waited and then just stepped onto it. *Now that was luck,* he thought.

Five done, he thought, and looked for his next target hand.

The next one was an up and down hand he wanted. There it was, just coming up from the black depths.

The hand he was on was moving away from it and Scott waited for it to stop and start its return.

At last it started its return journey and Scott saw that the hands would pass quite close to each other as they both met half way.

Scott moved to the fingers of the hand he was on and readied himself to jump onto the rising hand he needed next.

As it rose in front of the fingers on the hand he stood on, Scott jumped onto it and watched the hand he had stood on pass below the rising hand Scott now stood on.

Now a side to side one, he thought.

He was secretly pleased with his progress, this challenge wasn't so very hard and provided he didn't take unnecessary risks, he could finish quite quickly.

Unknown to him, he was going to regret that thought, for as he was part of the house for the moment, the house knew exactly what was going on in his mind!

Scott looked for his next hand moving side to side.

The hand he was on started its descent towards the black void as Scott looked for his next ride to the door.

He found it on the far side, moving very slowly away from him. I am going to have to go down to the bottom, he thought as he descended and saw the hand he wanted stop and then start to return.

Soon he lost sight of the hands altogether and sat on his hand in the middle. It began to get very cold and soon Scott was shivering.

The hand stopped and started to rise and Scott looked up and saw light above him, and slowly, he made out shapes of the other hands. Still very cold, he stood up and looked for the side to side hand he wanted. There it was, still very slowly moving across, above him.

The hand he was on moved on up and Scott gauged the timing to make the crossover to the slow hand. The hand he was on was coming up ever closer to the hand crossing over and Scott realised that it would pass over the hand he was on with very little clearance.

He lay down on the hand he was on and pressed himself as flat as he could. The hand passed over him and Scott sprang up and ran to the fingers of the hand he was on and jumped onto the slow moving hand as it moved away.

He landed safely and started to look for his next hand.

The next one was to be another up and down one.

He saw the one he needed but it was on its way down and he was on a slow hand. He sat on the palm of the hand and waited for this hand to start back the other way. He kept his eye on the hand he needed next and thought it was going quite fast.

It reached the end of its journey down and started back up. The hand Scott sat on was still slowly moving away to the side.

At last, the hand Scott was on stopped and started back.

Scott became aware that the hand he was on was not going to get near enough for him to jump onto the next one, and he would have to wait for it to go up and down again before he could be near enough to jump on it.

He sat again and watched his target hand start its descent once again.

He kept looking at the gap closing and thought that if the up and down hand went up once more, then he might be near enough to jump onto it as it came down next time.

It passed in front of the hand Scott was on and went on up. Scott stood up and waited for the hand to come down. As the two hands drew closer, the hand coming down, Scott thought, would pass behind the hand he was on. He moved to the fingertips of the hand he was on and as the other one dropped behind, Scott just dropped a short way onto it. Perfect timing.

Just two more to go he thought. The hand continued down, then returned back up quite quickly.

Scott saw the next hand he wanted and worked out that the hand he was on would go up and down and up once more before the next hand was close enough to jump on to. This proved correct and after the moves he predicted, the ninth hand was moving close enough to drop onto as it passed under the hand he was on.

Scott watched the fingers appear below him as he looked down from the hand he was on. He dropped onto the palm of the hand and stood up looking for his last hand ride. It was just rising from below the hand he was on and, as the hand was moving away, he would need to wait. He looked at the door so very close now and thought that it would be soon over. The hand he sat on moved to the end of its sideways journey and started to return. Scott looked at the next hand, the last hand he would use to get to the exit door, and gauged the timing to jump on to it.

As it rose up, Scott could see that it would rise up first but as it came down, he should be able to transfer to it.

He watched it rise, then begin to descend. He stepped onto it as it passed in front, dropping down.

Scott waited until it rose again and stepped from it onto the stone in front of the door. He was just going to step onto the red stone to end the challenge when he noticed writing on the open palm of the door. It read:

PLACE THE KEY IN MY PALM

"What key," he said.

He looked around the floor, all about the frame of the door but could see no key. He knew if he stepped on the red stone, the quest was over and he had failed, how close he had come to that!

He turned around and looked back to the door he had entered by, and there, hanging on the door was a large key.

Shaking his head, Scott looked back at all of the hands, still moving up and down or side to side.

"Okay, I failed to look behind me as I entered the room and that's my fault," said Scott, "it's back to the beginning—at least I am still in play."

He stepped towards the edge and waited for the hand to rise so that he could reverse his way back. He was angry with himself; he had been advised to look around before starting but had not looked at the door behind him.

If he could get back over, get the key without stepping on the red stone, and return, he would be done with the room.

He didn't want to think that now he would do the travel on the hands twice more just to get back to his current position.

He stepped onto the hand and watched for the side to side one to get near him.

Slowly, he made his way back and again suffered the deep, deep cold on the hand that had dropped so low.

After a long time, catching the hands he needed to take him back to the beginning, he made it to the start platform but did not stand on the red stone. This would be the end of the quest, just as if he had given up, and no way was that going to occur!

He put his toes close to the red stone and then leaned in to the door. Resting one hand on the door he twisted slightly and reached up to the key. He just managed to get the bottom of the key and then stood on tip toes to unhook the key. He had it. He pushed himself away from the door and turned to the start once again.

Glancing back at the door in case another key had appeared, he looked for the first hand to take him on his way.

The key had a large ring on it and Scott tried it over his head, it dropped nicely on to his neck and hung on his chest.

"Great, that leaves my hands free to help when I need to jump," he said.

He stepped onto the first hand moving side to side and looked for the next one.

It was the one that moved up and down fast and as he saw it, he readied his self to jump onto it.

He waited and just at the right moment jumped onto the rising hand.

Scott would never be sure if it was the key that caused him to flip as he jumped, or if he totally mistimed the jump but he missed most of the hand and rolled to the finger's edge and fell.

As he rolled over the edge, he grabbed at the finger and managed to hold on.

He was now hanging on by one hand.

Scott tried to swing a little to get his other hand on the fingers and on the second attempt he found a hold but he was now quite weak, his hands hurting with the strain of hanging on and he was almost at the point of tears with the strain.

He had almost done it, and now it would soon be all over.

The hand he hung on raised to its maximum height and started down.

Scott glanced down and saw the hand that would be his next hand moving slowly under the hand he was descending on.

As it got near, Scott let go and dropped onto it as it slowly passed below the hand he had been hanging on. Again, he remembered to not stand up as he passed under the hand he had jumped from.

No doubt about it, Scott was lucky—he was back in the quest!

He was on the third hand and looking for the fourth, this time he thought, I will take a lot more care.

This he did and slowly but very surely he reached the platform and lifted the key from around his neck.

He stepped up onto the red stone and placed the key onto the hand on the door.

The hand closed around the key and withdrew into the door itself and a handle appeared to the side.

Scott pressed it down and opened it and stepped out on to the landing at the top of the stairs. He almost shed tears of relief. That had been a very scary room, but had looked so easy.

The boys came running up the stairs to him shouting his praises for completing the room.

"What did you have to do; was it a scary room?" and other questions were also asked of him. When they quieted down, Scott started to tell them of his quest and how he had almost lost out.

He turned to the door when he came to the part of the key going into the hand and saw the door finishing the painting of itself with lots of hands in colours all over the black of the deep cold drop.

As he shivered at the thought, tiny white dots appeared on the door, just as if it were snow or frost.

Scott turned to the boys and said, "I did think I had lost, when I fell from the hand I aimed for, but I was lucky and let's hope I will be just as lucky in the next room. How many have I done now?"

"You have completed six now, Scott," said One.

"Am I ever going to know your real names at all?" asked Scott.

"Okay, Scott, you should know the truth," said One. "We just don't remember at all. We do know the order we arrived here but dates or years—we have no idea. We can't remember what clothes we were wearing and if we have brothers, sisters or Mothers or Fathers."

"But I remember all of this," said Scott. "I know that my mobile phone has gone, my pockets are empty now, and this has only happened since the front door closed."

"But you are not the full part of the house yet. You fail any quest and, like us, all memory will disappear; the house must think there is no need for it, just like food, or sleep. We don't know how old we are, I being One or the first, could be 200 years old, or just 15, we have no idea."

"This is why you are all dressed alike then, is it?"

"Yes, Scott, it must be, but with luck you will avoid becoming one of us, waiting for the house to open the front door for the next boy to enter."

"What's a mobile phone?" asked Two.

"That's a question I would also would like to have an answer to," said One.

"If I win on this quest, I will explain," said Scott.

"You have a lot of things we want to learn about, we hope you succeed on the quest, and then we might have a chance to compare our lives," said Three.

"Well, I had better get on with the next quest then," he said and moved to the next door; to the hand-painted door.

"This one is as good as any. I have no idea what's behind the door by just looking at it, so it will do."

Scott looked at the boys and turned to the door, took hold of the handle and pressed it down.

Chapter 9
The Seventh Quest

He opened the door and stepped in onto the red stone. He moved sideways as the door closed. He looked back this time but it was just a dull brown door, no keys on it.

In front of him were ten brown doors set in a wall.

How strange, ten doors in this puzzle also.

Scott could not think why he needed to wait any longer and stepped down on to the platform. He was in play!

He walked along the doors in front of him until he came to the end.

A sheer drop at the edge showed him that he could not go around.

He checked the other end and found it to be the same, no way around again.

"So I must go through the doors," he said.

He selected a door and opened it, and looked in.

In front of him were some stairs going up. He went in and started to climb the stairs. At the top was another open space with a wall with ten doors.

The doors were painted all sorts of colours.

Crazy, thought Scott.

He chose a blue door and opened it, a long corridor was in front of him.

He started along it and heard a rumble behind him. Stopping, he turned around and then turned and ran. The floor he had stepped on was falling into space. He rounded a corner and saw the opening. Still running, he reached the opening and stepped in onto the open platform just as the floor gave way under his other foot. He pulled himself in with no great effort, then turned to see what was next.

He was back where he had started from.

He again looked at the ten brown doors. No clue was to be found on the outside.

He turned back to the door he had come in by.

On the wall was a rhyme, he had not noticed it before but he thought it had appeared after he had tested the first lot of doors.

Scott moved over to read the wording; it may help in his quest.

What he saw was this:

> Once this quest has begun,
> In some corridors you must run,
> Some stairs will help, up or down,
> As will doors coloured brown,
> Ten times succeed upon this quest,
> Will give you then, your success,
> If you fail, this house you stay,
> So test all doors to find your way.

Scott re-read the rhyme and tried to remember the bits that would help him.

Brown doors will help. He looked at the doors he would need to pick from. They were all brown.

Well, he said to himself, *they will all be good to start but if I pick a corridor I shall just have to run.*

Let's hope I get stairs.

He moved to the doors and chose the next door to his first door picked.

Scott opened the door and saw that this had stairs going down. So far, so good.

He descended the stairs and found he was on another open platform area with ten doors.

All of the doors were of different colours, and not one of them was painted brown.

Scott remembered that he had picked a blue door and that had been a dangerous corridor so he picked a yellow one.

Opening the door, he was pleased to see stairs going up.

He ascended the stairs and once again, found an open platform area.

In front of him were ten more coloured doors.

This time he had two brown doors amongst the others.

He felt confident as he opened one of the brown doors.

In front of him was a corridor. He stepped in and ran, but no rumble followed him. He reached the open area and turned. The corridor was intact. He sighed, "This house catches me out so often."

He had now cleared three doors.

Scott looked at the next set of ten doors.

"No brown doors," he said out loud as he studied the doors.

He now looked for a yellow one—none!

Purple, orange, three black, one blue, and two white.

He picked the purple door and opened it. It was a slide. *Let's hope it's not a slide to the black hole*, he thought.

He got on and slid down the slide, faster and faster and then…

Landed on his bottom at the start.

Well, at least I didn't end up as part of the house, he thought.

Before starting again, he thought about the colours he had tried.

Blue was bad, yellow was good, as was brown, purple was back to the start.

He now knew how to get three doors done, so he decided to repeat the route he had just done.

First, the brown door that gave him the stairs going down, then the yellow door with stairs going up. Now he came to the platform with the choice of two brown doors. If he took the other door, would it give him a better choice of colours or should he pick the same brown door as last time?

Scott decided to try the other brown door.

He moved over and opened it. This time in front of him were stairs going upwards.

Scott climbed the stairs and came to the next platform of ten doors.

As he looked, he counted the colours.

No brown doors, no yellow doors. Two blue doors, one pink, three black, one purple, one orange and two green doors.

The blue doors were unhelpful and dodgy. The purple door put him back at the beginning. This left a choice of any of the seven in front of him that were left. Black, orange, green or pink.

He was about to open one of the green doors when he had a thought.

Pink, why pink? Boys would hate pink and would not normally pick it.

He moved along the row of doors to the pink door and opened it.

In front of him were stairs going up.

"Yes," said Scott punching the air.

He stepped onto the first step and started his way up, pleased that he had found a safe one.

Then he heard the rumble and immediately started to run up the stairs—it was clear this was not a safe choice.

He bounded up but found that as he came near to the top, the step he was on was already falling.

His heart was beating faster and faster as he struggled up the last few steps but he was losing. He dived for the gap, taking a chance that he would make it.

He had nothing to lose. He slid along the platform as he felt the stairs fall away.

Just like a goalie, he thought, as he slid along the floor of the platform coming to a stop just before a door.

His knees were scraped as were his elbows.

He stood up and looked at the doors. One brown, two green, one black, one blue, one purple, one white, one orange and two red.

Scott felt he had one choice, the brown one.

He opened the door and saw a corridor in front of him. He stepped in and started walking, listened for any rumbles but none came. He took it easy as he walked along and turned the corner. He arrived at the next platform and sighed. He had now completed five doors with five to go.

Again, in front of him were ten doors, and the colours he noticed were one red, one blue, one violet, one green, one black, two grey, one white, and two orange.

No brown or yellow, thought Scott. *Now let me think, what ones can I discount as dead dodgy?*

The blue one is a dangerous one, but only that one,' he thought.

Red is a danger sign, so I think I will miss that, green is a go sign to cross the road safely, so that might be a good colour to pick. Black is like the black hole I could fall in if I pick that, so I will leave that. Grey is a mixture of black and white, this could be good or bad. White is a nice clean colour so this could be good. Orange is half red and half yellow, this again could be a chancy one, good one time, bad the next.

What to do, no clue to help other than his best guess. He decided to go for green, thinking that green was for go as per his prior thinking.

He moved to the green door and opened it.

In front of him were stairs going down.

He stepped in and started down. At last, he came to an end and found a corridor to his left. He started walking along it and at last came to another set of stairs going up. He climbed the stairs and came to the platform.

Behind him, a door slammed. He looked around him, it was the green door he had just gone through, he was back on the same platform he had just left.

"Well, at least I haven't gone back to the start again, but now I must make another choice."

He decided on the white door. He had reasoned that the White was a clean colour, so it might be a good one for him.

He opened the white door and found a curving corridor in front of him.

He ran into the corridor and around the bends, first to the left then to the right. Then the bend rose up and then down like bumps in a road. Finally, out of breath, he arrived at the new platform.

He turned to look back to see if anything had happened to the passageway but could see nothing—everything had disappeared.

Scott turned to look at the doors again on this new platform.

It would seem that white doors are friendly doors, he thought, *but now I have six doors done.*

Scott looked at the colours on the next set of doors. In front of him was very little choice, as seven doors were black, one was grey, one was purple, and one was pink.

"Well," said Scott, "pink is out as that is really dangerous; purple is out as that takes me to the start, so it's grey or black."

The house is keen for me to try black, with seven doors, he thought.

He decided to try the grey as he had convinced himself that it might be a safer door than black.He opened the door and saw squares in the corridor, first black then white then grey then black then white then grey repeating along to the opening in the distance.

"Why the colours?" he asked himself.

He stepped onto the black square and it started to break as it fell into the dark void below. Scott scrambled to get onto the white square as the black disappeared into the void. Scott was left hanging half on and half off of the white square. He pulled his left leg up and then, kneeling, pulled the right leg up. Soon he was standing on the White square.

"Well, black is bad for me, but what about grey?" he said out loud. The quest was beginning to get to him.

He looked at the grey square and then the black.

"I think I will run onto the grey square, jump onto the black square and then jump, as quick as I can, onto the white," he said again out loud.

Taking a deep breath, he ran onto the grey square then jumped onto the black square then jumped onto the White square. Safe again.

Just like a hop, skip and jump at school, he thought as he watched the black square fall in bits into the black void, and the grey square slowly crack then break and fall after the black one had gone.

So I now know that black is nasty, grey is fairly safe but not totally, and white as I found out before, is good, he thought.

He turned to look up the passageway of the corridor and, using the same system of hop, skip and jump, finished the corridor. He was now on the next platform of doors.

Seven doors done, not all as easy as they looked and some really scary.

Scott's legs and elbows were hurting from the dive he had done when he went through the pink door and had scraped his skin.

He looked at the eighth set of doors.

What colours did he have now?

One grey, two orange, one purple, one black, one green, one violet, one blue and two pink.

Let's discount the bad ones, he again said to himself.

Two pinks are no good, one black is also no good.

The blue is also out, and the green is also out as it returns me here. Purple takes me back to the start, so my choice left is two orange, one Violet and if I want to risk it, the grey one, that could have black and white also behind the door.

"I think I have only two options to pick on this and both are new colours to go through. Violet is close to purple and that took me to the beginning again. Could that be the same? Orange is a mixture of red and yellow, yellow was helpful but could red be bad? *Oh dear*, he thought, *this is getting so hard and I have got so far.*

He moved to the violet door, then back to the orange door.

He looked along the lines of colours and then having made a decision he walked up to the violet door and opened it.

In front of him was a ladder that was going straight upwards but although he looked, he could see no end.

He started to climb and kept up a steady pace going up and up. At last he saw a hole partway up, but the ladder went on up. Should he crawl into the hole? Where would it bring him? He looked up. Still no end in sight. *If, when I get up to the top nothing's there, I can always climb back down*, he thought.

Again, he had forgotten that the house was listening to his thoughts as well as any spoken thoughts. As he passed the hole, the ladder broke into bits below his foot but just above the hole, leaving no ladder near enough to get to the hole.

I guess I have no choice then but to go on climbing.

Scott climbed and climbed and slowly he came to an open space. Seven tunnels went from the open space, over each was a number, not in order but all numbered up to seven.

Scott thought about his choice, and decided on five.

He walked into the tunnel and started to walk down in a circular route. After a short while, he came to a corridor and walked the short way to the new platform with ten new doors.

Scott was pleased that he had solved the puzzle of the seven numbers, and he thought if he did get back, he would ask the boys if they could solve it.

Scott had eight doors done now. He looked at the range of doors, and saw that the colours were quite a mixture. A new tone of colour was a magenta door, then an orange door, two black doors, a grey door, two red doors, a purple door and two blue doors.

Once again, Scott decided to sort out the doors he didn't want to go through based on his prior experience. The two black doors and the two blue doors were ruled out as dodgy. He ruled out the purple door also as that would take him back to the start. It was no to picking the grey door, as this was a mixture of two colours and had almost caused Scott to lose on the quest. He looked at the red doors; *this could be a problem,* he thought, as he had decided that this was a danger sign. So having ruled out eight doors he was left with two doors, the orange one and the new coloured door painted magenta.

He thought about magenta; how to make the colour, it was red and blue with another colour, but what?

Scott gave up and thought about the orange. This was a mixture of red and yellow. If it was like the corridor in the grey colours test, then yellow would be safe, red would be bad and orange would be a slower bad option. Should he go for it? His past thinking had got him this far, so it might just see him through.

He moved to the orange door and opened it. Just as the grey door had revealed, a corridor with three colours was in front of him. His first colour was the red, then the orange and then the yellow. This was repeated along the corridor from the entrance to he hoped, the last set of doors.

Scott thought about his attempt in the grey corridor and decided that red must be the bad colour and if it was like the grey, then once trod on, it would break and send him to the dark hole, orange slowly and yellow firm. He hoped he was going to be right on this thinking.

Hop, skip and jump, he thought.

He jumped onto the red, then onto the orange and then the yellow and stopped. He turned around and smiled, he had been right, the red step was gone, the orange one was just breaking and the yellow he was on was firm.

Scott continued his 'Hop, skip and jump' journey along the corridor and reached the tenth platform with no problems.

He looked at the doors, just two on this last stage. One door was painted gold, the other silver.

This was the last door to this quest, and he had to pick correctly—he had come so far.

Gold or silver? He wondered which one he should pick.

He went to the silver door. With fingers crossed, he opened the door and stepped onto the landing then looked back as the door closed.

He was next to the door with the hands painted on it that he had finished last time.

The door began to paint itself and lots of coloured doors appeared in the painting.

Scott turned and looked down the stairs, as shouting boys ran up to him.

"What happened? What did you do? Great to see you back," and lots of other excited questions.

Scott held up his hands and said, "Let me sit on the stairs and I will be able to tell you about the room's challenge."

The boys went down and sat on the stairs, and looked up at Scott.

Scott sat down at the top, looking down, then started to relate the way he had worked out the route to get to finish the quest.

The boys sat listening and gasped as he told them how the black square fell away as he stepped on it and how the grey one cracked and also fell away.

He then felt his elbow and knee. Everything was back to normal, even his trousers were repaired. Scott asked about the seven numbers and explained that the colours of the rainbow were seven and as he was safe with a yellow door then it was the fifth tunnel he should take.

When he came to the gold or silver doors, they asked why he had picked the silver door and not the gold.

"I decided that the house would like to be the winner, so as silver was a second place, I decided that I would open that door."

All the boys said that they would have gone through the gold door.

Scott looked down at them and smiled, "Yes, I almost did, but the house has won already with me inside and not able to get out, so I may as well accept it."

Scott then stood up, he again looked at his hands, rubbed his eyes and said, "I cannot get used to this, I feel just as I did when I came into the house, quite full of energy. I have climbed, ran, jumped and lifted planks in all of the rooms and yet I am not tired. Weird!" He looked at the boys still sat on the stairs and said, "Well, Three, you and I are equal now on the rooms done, I think it's time to start the next one." He stepped back upstairs and picked the next door and, nodding to the boys who had followed him up, he turned and opened the door.

Chapter 10
The Eighth Quest

Scott stepped in and moved sideways as the door closed behind him. He looked down at the red stone and turned and looked at the door he had entered by. No key!

In front of him was what looked like a maze, it seemed to be split into three parts as Scott could see one third was made from bricks, then the next was a thorn hedge, and the last looked like a river. In the distance was a waterfall pouring into the river.

The door was on top of the waterfall.

How was he going to reach that?

Bridges could be seen rising over parts of the maze, and Scott thought this was most likely the way he would travel from one section to another.

In front of him were three openings in the brick wall, all being a first stage of the maze.

Before he stepped down, Scott looked for any clues. He saw that some writing was on a wall to the side of the red stone but the angle was wrong for him to read it. He would need to get down from his safe place to read it.

He stepped down and moved at an angle to read the message. This is what he read:

Danger this quest by design,
Just to make sure you are mine,
but three chances, you, I gave.
To succeed, you must be brave.
Cross a bridge to beat all three,
The door to home, you shall see.

Whatever is that all about? thought Scott. He turned and looked at the maze again and as he did, he saw a head pop up just above the brick maze. It was a dinosaur. *Oh dear,* thought Scott. *The house has done it again! It's determined to get me killed.*

He watched the head pop up again near the left hand entrance, and so ran to the far right entrance, entered and continued running until he came to a junction.

He looked back to the entrance in time to see a wall build across the gap. He was now securely in the maze with a dinosaur!

He turned back to the junction. Left or right? He turned right and started running again. He could hear lots of heavy breathing in front of him and slowed down.

As he came to a corner, he saw the head of the dinosaur just looking over the brick wall he was going along.

It seemed to be trying to get into Scott's pathway but couldn't, as something seemed to be stopping it from climbing over. Just its head was able to reach over. Scott became aware that a clear roof was placed over the maze and was set to stop the dinosaur and maybe keep him from climbing over. Advancing slowly he came to the part where the dinosaur was still struggling to get to Scott. He ducked down very low and crawled passed it, then standing up, he ran on and around another bend.

He could hear the dinosaur roaring behind him and turned another corner to cause him to go back towards the dinosaur. *I hope this is not going to bring me into its lane,* thought Scott, whose heart was pounding in his chest.

This is really scary, he thought. He walked very slowly to the next bend and then looked around the corner. No, the dinosaur was not in this part of the maze that he was on. Scott decided to jog along this straight bit of wall until he came to another turn or junction. Suddenly, the dinosaur's head came over the side again, but this time on the opposite side. Scott skidded to a stop, he had such a fright as the dinosaur's head came over, scaring him—he had jumped back against the wall away from the beast!

"Oh my goodness," said Scott, "the house really is trying to get me. That almost scared me to death."

Taking a big breath, Scott got on hands and knees and crawled below the dinosaur who was doing its best to get to Scott. As Scott came below the dinosaur, a great blob of saliva-like jelly dropped onto his head.

Scott jumped again and crawled faster until he knew he was clear, then he stood up. He reached up and pulled huge handfuls of slimy saliva from his hair and his neck as it slipped down. More slid down over his face and he just managed to stop it going into his eyes. What was even more revolting, it stunk of bad eggs!

"He doesn't clean his teeth at night," said Scott out loud as he started on his way. *I think the dinosaur is in an end of the maze and he may now turn and follow me in the hope that our paths cross*, he thought.

Scott picked up his pace, jogging along until he came to a junction. Right or left? He had started with the right hand entrance so he decided to stay with that. Turning right he saw a head moving along the maze in front of him, but it looked as if there was two lanes separating him from the dinosaur. He hoped so.

Moving toward the dinosaur he watched it turn in its lane and pass back in front of Scott but now, only one lane separated them.

The dinosaur stopped and looked at Scott. He pushed his head over the wall and gave a great sniff. Scott stood still. The dinosaur then snorted and blew out of his mouth and a great blob of slime flew towards Scott.

Scott jumped to the side as the blob landed next to him. "It spat at me and now it's blowing nasty bogies at me," he said out loud, then realised he was talking to himself again.

The head withdrew and Scott moved carefully around the smelly bogie that was beginning to spread across the path.

He moved up to where the head of the dinosaur had been, then turned to go alongside the lane the dinosaur was in.

As he walked slowly along watching the top of the wall he noticed that he was going down slowly. He stopped and looked at his route, no doubt about it—it was a downward slope and it was getting deeper.

He turned a bend and saw the slope went down to take him below a maze path and then it looked as if it went back up.

Scott walked on until he got to the bridge and stopped as he heard a roar. Great feet stamped on to the bridge above his path and then the Dinosaur's head poked over the top. It licked its lips as it looked at Scott. Scott ran under the bridge as fast as he could and kept running around one bend then another. At last, he slowed down slightly out of breath. No sound could be heard behind him and so he walked slowly on to the next junction which was again a T junction. Again, he stayed with the right hand turn. He started along the path and after a short while came to a bend. As he started to go around it, he saw a head rise above the wall just ahead of him. The dinosaur was in the same lane as him now.

Turning around, Scott quietly made his way back to the junction and went straight on. Behind him came a roar and then a snort.

Scott started running along the maze path away from the dinosaur that was now coming after him.

He ran around a bend and then started to run upward. At last, he was above the maze and in front of him was a bridge that went over the river and descended into the thorn maze. Scott ran as fast as he could and soon got onto the bridge. The dinosaur was just behind him, but Scott was now descending to the thorn maze.

Scott looked behind him as he ran down and then slowed down—the dinosaur could come no further.

A huge gate had appeared and blocked its way.

Thank goodness for that, but what am I going to encounter in this part? he said to himself.

Scott delayed starting the next maze as he wanted to get his breath back and to calm down. His heart was pounding in his chest and when he held his hand out, it was shaking very badly.

Once he felt calmed down, he started on his way. He followed the path he was on as it was the only path available to him until he came to any junction.

He was looking at the thorn bushes making the maze up and marvelling at the coloured flowers on it. One huge red one caught his eye in the next lane in front of him and it seemed to be moving.

Scott stopped and watched it. It stopped also!

Standing quite still, Scott studied the flower. He took one step along the path, the flower moved also.

He picked up a small stone from the path and threw it over the hedge. As it fell making quite a lot of noise, the flower moved very fast towards the sound. It was attracted by sound. *This could be my next enemy,* thought Scott, *but what can a moving flower do that is worse than a dinosaur?*

When it got to the place where Scott had thrown the stone, a sound like a cough came to Scott and then green vapour started to filter through the hedge.

Scott moved away as quietly as he could, holding his breath, until he was away from the flower. If the vapour smells as bad as the dinosaur's spit, he didn't need to smell it! He then smelt his hands and said aloud, "I stink from the dinosaur's spit."

He followed the path and further on saw another red flower again over the hedge on the other side.

He looked for a stone again and picked it up. Again he tossed it over the hedge, behind where he was stood while standing still. When the stone clattered onto the path over the hedge, the red flower seemed to rush to the sound.

Scott moved forward away from the area the red flower was. As he moved away, he heard the same cough sound. Looking back, he saw green vapour coming through the hedge once again.

He turned around a bend in front of him and came to a fork junction. He had three choices, turn right, turn left or go straight on.

Nothing gave him any idea which one to pick so he went straight on.

He walked for quite a while until he came to a big open area. The path went around the open grass area both ways and joined again directly across from the entrance Scott stood at.

In the middle were rabbit holes and now and then, a rabbit popped up and started to eat dandelion leaves and daisies.

As he watched, a red flower came up behind where he was standing and Scott quickly stepped to the side of the hedge keeping his back to the hedge.

He held his breath as the flower came out of the lane and moved onto the grass.

It was walking on its roots!

Scott breathed out quietly, but stayed motionless for he was convinced that the flower could not see, but was attracted to noise, but why?

He was about to find out!

As Scott studied the flower, he noted that it seemed to have eye sockets but no eyes. Just above the roots was a huge bright red wobbling 'belly' and growing up its huge long neck was lots of funny coloured leaves growing in a circle around it.

The flower moved over to the rabbit holes and then stopped. After a short time, a rabbit popped up and started to move around eating a leaf here and there. As it neared the stationary flower, the flower started to drop its head.

Scott watched as it got closer to the rabbit, and then the cough came. The rabbit was covered in the green vapour, and tried to run out of it but, it was falling all over the place.

It's killed it with the vapour, thought Scott.

The rabbit gave one last kick of its leg and lay still. The flower moved over to it, lifted its roots over the rabbit and sank down on it.

Scott moved slowly around the green, watching the flower, but if it heard Scott it made no move towards him—it was eating the rabbit!

Scott got to the other side and made his way to the lane, entered it and started on his way to wherever it would take him. He followed the path, turning bends to the left and right and then came across another big open area. In it was a group of yellow flowers. They looked just like the red flowers, the only difference being the yellow flower.

As Scott came into the area, looking around he could see that this also had a path going around the green area, and meeting directly opposite the entrance where Scott now stood.

The flowers were all on the green, and had made no movement towards Scott. Keeping as quiet as he could, he stepped onto the grass at the edge of the path and, walking on the grass, slowly walked around the pathways grassy edge towards the exit on the other side.

He had reasoned that the grass would keep the noise down, but as he moved around from the entrance he also became aware that the flower heads moved around with him, almost as if they were watching him!

He had got about a third of the way around, when a red flower came in to the area where Scott had entered, and turned towards Scott.

Scott kept still and quiet, still on the grass edge, still two thirds of the way to go to get out of the grassy circle. The red flower moved to the grass and seemed to push one root into the ground. It then turned towards Scott. Scott didn't wait—he ran. Yellow flowers were spaced across the grassland, the red flower was behind him. He raced as fast as he could along the path, not worrying about the noise on the stone path. He just needed to get out of here.

The red flower caught up with him as he almost made it halfway around and, with one root, tripped him up.

As Scott struggled to get up, he heard the cough, and green vapour covered him. He got to his feet and tried not to breathe any in, as he rushed as best he could across the grass to get away. It was no good, he had to breathe. He knew he had lost, as he sucked in air and the green vapour. He felt his legs go wobbly as he staggered out of the mist, almost bumping into a yellow flower. As Scott fell to the ground, his power gone from his legs and body, he became aware of another movement in front of him. He couldn't move now, he just wanted to sleep, as the red flower came into view to the side of him.

The red flower's root lifted over Scott and he felt it brush across him. He was very sleepy and all feeling was slowly going from his body.

An orange vapour covered his body and eyes and he breathed it in. He could do nothing but just lay there and await his fate. As he lay there, he became aware that feeling was slowly returning, and he felt the red flower's root pull away from his body.

The orange vapour slowly cleared and, still lying on the grass, he watched the red flower go away from where he lay, and go back down to the entranceway where both he and it had entered this grass plain.

As the feeling came back to him, Scott lifted his head and turned slightly to look around. Behind where he lay were two yellow flowers with some roots out of the ground that seemed to be in a circle around him. *Am I going to be eaten by yellow flowers instead of a red flower?* he asked himself.

Nothing moved as the feeling in Scott's legs at last returned, and unbelievably, he felt almost back to normal—whatever normal was in this house.

He pushed himself up and sitting on his bottom, looked up at the yellow flowers in front of him. One lowered its head towards him and then, as if it had looked at him and could see he was better, withdrew its roots and turned and walked away to the centre of the grass plain. A moment later, the other flowers followed. Scott watched the last flower push its roots into the ground and then stretch out its leaves to the sun above.

"Weirder and weirder," muttered Scott as he stood up.

He realised that the yellow flowers had saved him from the red flower's vapour, and that the yellow flowers had covered him with the orange vapour that had restored the strength to his body. They had saved his life, he had not lost after all!

At first he was not very steady on his feet, but as he made his way to the exit, he watched the yellow flowers just in case!

At last he came to the exit and with his legs almost back to normal, stopped and looked back.

The yellow flowers were all turned towards him. Could they be watching him?

Just in case, Scott waved to them and moved into the gap and continued down the path away from the second grass plain he had come to. No doubt about it, Scott was lucky.

The path took him to an upward slope and as he came to the crest he could see that he was coming to a bridge over the river and it then dropped down on the other side.

He must have completed two parts of the maze, thanks to the yellow flowers.

He crossed the river and descended to the path on the other side. Following the path he turned a corner and dropped slowly down. His feet were getting wet and turning the next corner, Scott stopped as he found the path was no more. In front of him was water; the path had become a river.

Scott could go no further forward other than going into the water, He looked at the sides of the river bank, but the thorn bush just went into the water, stopping him going anywhere else.

What about my clothes? he thought. His shoes were already wet—going back was no option—so should he just jump in and swim?

He bent forward and felt the water. It was warm—quite pleasant really. *Okay,* thought Scott, *I have no choice*, and he stepped into the water expecting to sink down, but he found that the path was still beneath his feet but he couldn't see it. The water was a murky brown and, as he walked, he descended lower and lower into the water. The thorn bush on both sides raised up on a bank giving no chance for him to avoid his current course as he slowly walked deeper into the water.

Soon he was up to his neck in the water and he had to swim or struggle to walk, bobbing along by thrusting forward. The water had now cleared and Scott could see almost to the bottom.

On the sides of the river was now a bank, the thorn bush now behind him. Scott decided to try to climb onto it to get out of the water. As he caught hold of the grass edge and heaved himself up, he bumped his head against a clear barrier. He could not get out onto the narrow lip at the side of the river, the house had that sorted—he had to swim.

What he did see as he lifted his body up, was lots of narrow channels filled with water and some bridges in the near distance over the river.

He lifted himself up again to take another look through the clear barrier, being careful not to knock his head this time. Yes, it was a maze of water channels and in the distance, he could see the waterfall and the door at the top.

He dropped down and began to swim along the river, aware that his clothes were wet and dragging him down. He continued for some time swimming around corners and at one point an L-shaped corner, but he was getting tired. His shoes and clothes were soggy and pulling him down.

He felt the ground below him brush his knee and realised that he should be able to stand. As he put his feet down, he stood and found that he could stand but again the water had become muddy brown and he could not see the bottom.

The water was just above his waist. The prickly thorn bush was back again and obscured his view of what was on the other side. He walked through the water and around a bend. In front of him was a bridge, and as he waded towards it, so the ground rose as did the bank with the thorn bush on it.

Scott walked onto the bridge and stopped. He leaned on the rails and rested for a while. He then noticed a movement in the water across the different channels of water, and it gave him quite a shock.

A big black triangle was moving along the channel, it was about five channels away from where he stood.

As he watched, it came to an intersection and after a pause, turned round a corner and followed its chosen route, towards where Scott was! Scott knew that with his wet clothes on, he wasn't going to have much chance to get away. "Sorry, Mum," he said aloud and quickly took his shoes, socks, shirt and trousers off, and dropped them onto the bridge. His bicycle helmet had disappeared when he had come into the house and the door had shut. In the confusion of the moment, his only thought had been his mobile phone.

He now stood in his pants—one of his favourites with footballs all over it.

He walked over the bridge and watched the black fin pass under the channel that his clothes were dripping into. The fin stopped and did not move until Scott turned and walked into the water on the other side. He was now two channels away from the shark, for that was what Scott thought it was. As the ground sank, the thorn bush bank gave way again to the grass bank and Scott began to swim. He had a steady stroke, now very much easier than the first time, with his clothes on.

He swam around bends and came to a junction. Treading water, he thought about his view of the shark coming to a junction like this. It had turned towards him, so he swam in the other direction, still unable to see where he was going. Above him on the grassy bank was again the thorn bush, obscuring his view on both sides.

He swam along at a steady pace and came yet again to a junction, this was a crossway. He remembered that in the flower path, he had gone straight on, so he decided to do this again.

He swam across the junction and still keeping a steady rate, rounded a corner. In front of him was yet another bridge rising up out of the water, he had not seen it as he swam because of the thick bush on each side. As he reached the shallower water, he stood and started to wade towards the bridge. Behind him he heard a thrashing, and fear hit his heart as he rushed to the bridge. He pulled himself up out of the water and ran up onto the bridge.

Behind him the shark was almost out of the water, thrashing in the shallows trying to reach Scott. Scott rested on the bridge and let his heart slow down, he had quite a fright as he became aware that the shark had almost caught him.

After a short time, he walked up the bridge and looked back at the shark, still thrashing around, but slowly getting back into the water.

Scott crossed three channels as he walked over the bridge but although this gave him cause to be pleased, as he would be still in front of the shark. He was also shocked to see his clothes just as he had left them on the last bridge.

Was he on the same bridge? He could not be sure. He looked around. No, he was on a new bridge; the views were different. He lifted his trousers, still soaking wet, and looked at the rest of his clothes. Yes, it was his, and they were just as he had dropped them, expecting to not see them again. He folded the trousers as his Mother had told him to do, and placed them on the bridge. He then sorted the rest out into a folded pile and lastly placed his shoes to the side of the neat pile of clothes.

He felt better for doing this, but then became aware that the shark was gone. *I wonder if he can smell me*, he thought, then realised that, since going into the water, he no longer smelt of dinosaur spit— it had all washed from his hair and body.

He sniffed his clothes and they also had no bad smell, they had been washed by the first swim.

Scott suddenly thought about the shark and looked around, there, swimming towards him under the bridge, was the shark. The shark was now only one channel away from the lane Scott would need to go in. Scott ran down the slope of the bridge and into the water and started to swim, he again kept a steady stroke and a short time later came to another junction, this time a fork. He took the left one and swam on.

Below him he saw a large fish swimming along and then another. They seemed to be more afraid of him and as he passed over them, they turned and swam back the way he had come. Scott rounded a bend and came to an overhanging rocky cliff. As he swam, the rocks gradually closed over him, and soon he was swimming in a tunnel. He swam on and then just in front of him, he saw that the rock came down to the top of the water and went deeper.

Scott looked back in case the shark was closing in on him.

He couldn't go back as it must be behind him, so taking a huge lung full of air, he dived down under the water and turning onto his back reached up to the rock's top and kicking with his legs, he pulled his way along by grabbing handholds on the rock's surface.

At last he felt the rock moving upwards and swam faster as he saw daylight. He broke the surface and exhaled then took another deep breath.

He was in a cave but he could see steps coming from the water. He swam over and stepped out onto a small platform. In front of him was a dark corridor that he decided he would take, as he didn't want to swim under water again. He could see that where the cave dropped into the water again, a tunnel could be seen just like the one Scott had come through, with a dull light showing through.

He was just going to turn when the tunnel became quite dark and then the black fin rose in the cave. Scott had been swimming towards the shark!

If he had not got out of the water, he would now be a statue waiting for the next boy to come in the door.

The fin moved slowly around the cave and then a tail broke the surface as it seemed to dive down. A moment later, a snout and evil eyes broke the surface and great jaws opened as a big fish, like the ones Scott had seen below him, was dropped down the throat of the shark.

It sank down and then turned again in circles waiting for its next meal to walk down the stairs into its mouth.

Scott shivered and turned and walked along the tunnel, his hands touching the sides to help guide him.

He wound his way upward and as he turned around the next corner, he saw daylight.

Scott came out onto another platform looking down on the maze. He could see below him the water maze, he could see bridges over the river channels and he could see the thorn bush maze. In the distance he could see the red flowers over the top of thorn bush pathways and also could see the brick maze. He could even see the Dinosaur's head sticking up in one of the brick maze paths.

Have I done so much? thought Scott, as he looked around.

He saw that a pathway led down from the ledge he was on and cautiously he walked down.

Slowly, he neared the waterway again, but as the path he was on followed to the base of the mountain, he saw that again it would lead him to yet another bridge. As he rounded the corner, he saw that he was close to the waterfall. He started to go up the slope of the bridge and stopped in the middle, never taking his eyes from the falls and the door hovering above it.

"Not so far away now," he said aloud, and walked on over the bridge. He nearly tripped over his clothes as he walked down the bridge slope on the other side. "This house never ends its surprises," he said as he made his clothes tidy once again. The room he was in now for its quest was just as if he was outside; the sun was shining, clouds drifted over now and then—it was like a summer's day. He could see miles and miles from on top of the bridge. Now, how to get to the waterfall? He looked for the shark but could not see it.

He ended crossing the bridge and stood by the water edge and looked back at his clothes that seemed to be following him on each journey. Scott shook his head and turned to the water in front of him, he walked in and once in deep enough, started swimming. He tried to see the waterfall but the hedge was back, obscuring his view. Swimming on, he came to a V junction and again decided to keep to the one that he felt would take him in the general direction of the waterfall. He swam on, aware that the shark was in the same water as him, and that it might know where he was even if Scott had no idea.

As he came to a bend, he heard a splash and stopped swimming. Could the shark be around the corner? What could he do?

He eased up to the edge of the bend and took a quick look. Sure enough, it was the shark but it was pointing the other way. In the narrow confines of the channel, it could not turn so it would need to swim on until it came to a junction to turn and come back. It was trying to go backwards as it must have become aware of Scott swimming along and it had passed a junction. It couldn't go backwards even as it thrashed around.

Scott swam around the bend then into the other channel. He pushed hard as he swam not knowing how far the shark would need to swim to allow it to turn. It could find a deep part in the channel. *All things are possible in this house*, thought Scott.

He could hear the waterfall and it was getting louder.

He swam around a bend and there it was, with no hesitation, Scott swam as fast as he could towards it and saw the red stone under the waterfall. He would need to swim through the falling water. He pushed his tired arms hard and touched the red stone as a splash behind him warned him his problem was just behind him.

Ducking down then pushing upwards, he pushed up onto the red stone just as the shark reached the stone. It had missed eating him, but only by a short margin.

He turned and looked at the wall. A red button was flashing in front of him and Scott pressed it. A noise above him caused him to look up and he saw the door descending down towards him through the waterfall.

Once it reached the red stone, it stopped and Scott pressed the handle down, opened the door and walked back onto the landing at the top of the stairs.

He had done it. Scott sank to the floor feeling exhausted, but as he looked down at his feet in front of him he noticed he had his clothes and shoes on, and strangely he was also dry!

The crazy house had dressed him and dried him, and he had felt nothing!

He turned and watched the door paint itself, blue sky with a brick wall and a Dinosaur looking over. Then a green grassy bank with a river running by it and it had even put the shark in. The last thing was two flowers on the grass—one red, one yellow. Quite a beautiful painting, thought Scott.

The boys were yelling as they came back up the stairs. Shouts of "Well done," and "Brilliant," echoed around as Scott was hugged by the boys.

Three shouted, "Eight, Scott, you've done eight."

Scott grinned and said, "With the help of yellow flowers!"

"Tell us about it please, Scott," said Three, and in response Scott moved to the top of the stairs and sat down. The boys followed and went down a few more steps, then sat down looking up at Scott.

He told the boys about the room—how big it was, the three mazes and the nasty things in them. He spoke of meeting the dinosaur but two of the boys just looked at each other, clearly not understanding. He explained that it was a giant lizard but still they looked at him not understanding. He pointed to the painting on the door. "Let's say it was a monster," said Scott. Big smiles told him they now had an idea. When he told them about it spitting slimy saliva they roared with laughter. He came to the flowers and the good ones and bad ones, and how lucky he was that the yellow ones squirted orange vapour on him to free him from being the red flower's meal. Then he came to the shark and how this was a man eating giant fish upon which the boys nodded in understanding. He remarked about how his clothes kept following him and how as he had come through the door, he was dressed and quite dry.

Again, One reminded Scott that every time he returned through the door he went in, he would be back to normal, just as he was before. He looked at the boys and moved to another door. "Time to start another door's quest," he said.

The boys looked at him, smiled and wished him luck.

Chapter 11
The Ninth Quest

Scott was pleased that he had got so far, but was determined to concentrate on the next quest and try to come back out of the door he had entered.

That was another strange thing about this house; he could travel what seemed like miles whilst in a room yet still come out the same door.

He pressed down on the selected door and entered into the room.

He looked down at the red stone and almost forgot to move sideways away from the door closing.

Remembering to do so, he stood on the red stone and stood still, unable to understand what had happened to him. His clothes had changed!

Scott was dressed in a thick fur coat, thick boots, thick socks and had a thick hood over his head.

He was all in white.

"What the heck is going on," asked Scott, "I am dressed in this stuff in a moment, as I pass into the room. How can this happen?"

He pulled the hood down and felt something hard on top, so took hold of it and realised that it was goggles. He pulled them off and then fitted them over his head so that they went over his eyes.

The outside glass looked brown, like sunglasses but as he looked around, it was as if it was clear glass. He took them off again and put them into a pocket.

He looked around. He was in what looked like a hut.

Not a lot of furniture was around, in fact, the hut had one table that was not very big, and one chair. On the wall of the hut he could see two pictures of what looked like animals.

A door was at the other end.

On the wall on the other side, two things like a tennis racket were hanging on a nail. These had leather straps on them and Scott thought he had seen people wearing them on TV in snow. Could there be snow outside the door that he could see at the end of the hut? Would he need to wear the snow shoes he could see?

He could see a sheet of paper on the table and decided that standing here wasn't going to get the quest done.

He stepped from the red stone into the hut and immediately heard a roaring sound outside of the hut.

This was not an animal sound, this was the sound of really bad weather.

He looked behind to see if a message was on the closed door but the door was no longer there, just a plain wall with a window.

"Weirder and weirder," said Scott.

The hut was shaking and was quite cold. He had not been aware of any of this as he had stood on the red stone.

He could see outside and it confirmed what he had thought, he was in a hut in a snowstorm and it was a blizzard outside, gusting at a very fast rate.

Scott moved to the table and picked up the sheet of paper. On it was a message that read like this:

Two snowy poles you will find,
In this quest are combined,
Journey then to find my door,
Fail and stay for ever more.
One chance I give, but beware,
Twill save but once against a bear.
Around your neck, the help is near,
Throw and run when bears appear.
Be brave, strong and much more,
To get to safety through my door.

Scott looked at the rhyme again and then undid his thick white coat.

Sure enough, a small amulet like a bear, hung around his neck on a thin cord. He had not been aware of it before.

"Bears, I met one of those in the cube, I wonder if it's outside the door now?"

Scott moved to the window and looked out. He couldn't see a thing. The snow was falling quite heavily and he could see very little outside. The snowflakes were very big and the hut he was inside was shaking quite a lot with the wind outside.

I am not going outside yet, he said to himself. *The snow outside is so heavy that I would not be able to see anything outside, or have any idea which way to go to get to the door.*

He moved to the two pictures.

One was of Penguins but they were moving. Suddenly one came up to the picture and made Scott jump.

The other was of a white bear. As Scott looked at it, it turned and started to run towards Scott.

Scott stepped away and both pictures became still again.

This really is a weird house, thought Scott.

He decided to try on the snowshoes just for fun while he waited, as people used skis now when travelling in snow. Not that Scott had tried it, but he had seen enough on TV when he watched the Olympics.

He unhooked the snowshoes from the wall and placed them on the floor.

Next, he placed his boot onto the first of the racket-like shoe and moved the slide to lock his furry boot heel onto the shoe. Next, he looped the leather strap across the shoe and made sure the heel was located in the leather strap at the back.

He lifted his foot and smiled. He had, by logic, worked out how to wear a snow shoe. He set about doing the same for the other foot. Once he had done both, he tried walking around.

They were awkward but he soon got used to walking with them on. He had to make sure he did not step on one of the shoes or he would trip himself up.

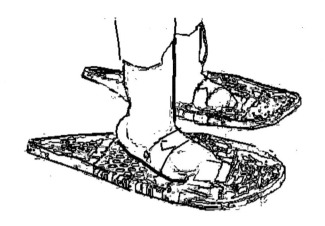

He looked out of the window and saw that the snow had stopped and the wind had dropped down while he had been trying the shoes on and practising the walking.

Still wearing the snow shoes, he did his coat up and walked to the door. If the bear was outside waiting, he wanted to know.

He opened the door slowly and looked out. No bear was near the door.

It was very cold and Scott pulled the hood up, then realised that he was squinting with the sunlight reflecting on the snow.

He backed into the hut and pushed the door shut. Next, he pulled his hood down, then pulled the goggles out of his pocket and fitted them. His hands were exposed, and had felt cold outside. What else was in the pockets?

He felt in another pocket and pulled out a thick pair of white gloves. Once he had them on he felt he was ready for the trek outside.

He opened the door again and looked out. Again, no bear.

He stepped onto the new snow and found that he did not sink into the snow which looked as if it might be deep.

It was a strange feeling walking with the snow shoes but he thought that the house had put them there to be used in this quest.

Once outside, he decided to walk up a sloping snow hill to look around, and see if he could see the door.

It was not easy and as he walked up to the crest, the shoes caused him to make a swinging action to walk as they were wider than his boots and in his practice, he had stood on them and nearly fallen over.

At last he reached the top and looked around.

He could see the hut below him and smiled at the strange oval footprints he had left coming up the hill.

As he looked the other way, he could see another hut in the distance. The route to the hut would be uneven but not too hard. He could go around some of the nasty bits.

Could the door be inside this? It can't be that easy, but he would need to check it out, he could see nothing else around him. He started on his way down and found it was just as hard with these snow shoes going down as it had been going up.

At last he was on level ground and this seemed a lot firmer.

He stopped and looked around, then bent and undid the strap to one snow shoe. Standing, he pressed down with the boot and found that it did not sink, it was hard underfoot with a layer of snow over it.

He bent and took the other snow shoe off and then tied them together.

By pulling the straps up an arm he could fit the leather ties onto a loop on the shoulder of his coat. This now was secure and the shoes hung on his back.

Scott set off again towards the hut. He seemed to be walking for a long time and still the hut seemed just as far away.

As he walked, he became aware of a lot of noise—something that he had never heard before.

He came to a slope of ice in front of him and realised he needed to go around it to see the hut again.

He had been going up and down over small slopes and this was the first time on his journey that he would need to go around something. As he moved around the ice, he found the source of the noise.

In front of him were a lot of penguins moving away from the rough ice where their nests were or returning to their partners who were sat on the nests in a rookery.

He watched the black and white birds waddling along, their black wings held out to help with the balance. He had seen them on TV but never like this, and he was grateful to the house for this chance.

He looked around as he suddenly remembered that he was on a quest, and as he had relaxed watching the birds, he could find that the house was lulling him into a relaxed state of mind as if on holiday, and bringing a problem up behind him in the shape of a bear.

Nothing! "Well thank you house," said Scott aloud, "it is a treat to see this in a true life situation, and much better than the picture."

Scott continued to watch for a little longer and then stepped around the ice block into full view of the penguins.

He started to walk towards the ones going or returning from wherever they went, thinking he could cut across their route without disturbing them.

The penguins had a different view. Scott might be a predator.

They ran in a group getting ever bigger as they came at him. Scott watched as he moved towards them thinking they were no real threat to him.

He was wrong—these were house penguins—and although they may look like normal penguins, they were aggressive.

The first ones that came near Scott suddenly dropped onto their fronts and used their feet to help keep the momentum forward, to knock into Scott.

The first one hit his leg and spun him around as the second one took his other leg giving him no chance to maintain his upright position.

He crashed down on his back onto the ice, and the oncoming penguins were on him at once.

They surrounded him and jabbed their beaks down at him. They hit his glasses and, although they didn't break with the continued attack, the front was getting very scratched.

Some turned their backs to him and bent over and squirted liquid fowl fish smelling poo at him.

Penguins pecked at his legs, pulling at the fur on his trousers and at his arms as he waved at them trying to push them away.

One jumped onto his belly and pecked between his thrashing legs.

Scott pulled up to a sitting position after the first strike from the one on his stomach, and pushed it off shouting, "Leave my willy alone!"

He pushed and punched as the Penguins started to attack his neck, now in easy reach. Still they squirted poo at him. It was on his face, his arms, his hood and his coat.

Scott pushed up onto one leg and then stood, and began to swing his arms knocking penguins to the floor or into others, as they arrived.

Slowly, he made a path through the Penguins who continued to try to stop his progress.

Scott saw two drop down onto their belly, and start to propel themselves towards him. They wanted to knock him down again, but as they got near, Scott jumped onto one of the backs of the sliding penguins, and jumping high from its back, landed into a group coming behind the sliding penguins. Lots fell and knocked others over just like skittles, as Scott landed on the ice again, and this gave him a chance to get away.

He pushed two penguins away, one on each side, and ran through the gap.

Others coming towards the mass, swerved away as he ran towards them. They needed a group and one or two was going to be no match against this predator.

Scott kept going and soon no penguins were in front of him. He was through!

He slowed down and looked around. His goggles were very scratched and he couldn't see very well through them with the poo and the scratches.

He lifted them up and tried to look around him without them but the reflection from the sun and enhanced light hurt his eyes.

He pulled the goggles down and looked back at the Penguins. They were back to their routine of going and coming as when he had first seen them.

It seemed but a moment ago when he had been admiring the penguins, but how things can change when you least expect it.

"And I thanked the house for letting me enjoy watching them. They tried to kill me," he said out loud.

He started back on his route towards the hut and slowly, he could see he was getting near.

Then the snow started. At first, it was a few flakes, then, within a short time, he was in a blizzard.

If this came down at home he thought he would be happy, but not now. It was coming down so fast and thick he could hardly see the hut.

Trying to keep a straight line he trudged on keeping his head down against the blowing snow.

The wind was now very strong and was causing him to have trouble to keep the line he needed.

He looked up but couldn't see the hut. Everything was white in front of him.

He leaned into the wind and plodded on. The snow was getting thick underfoot and he was beginning to struggle to lift his feet with each step. Snow seemed to be coming over the top of his boots.

Should he stop and try to put the snow shoes on again? He felt behind him and could feel them still there. They may have broken when he fell on his back. If he had stopped and tried to put them on and they might have had broken in the Penguins' attack, then he would have wasted his time.

He trudged on, getting slower and slower.

He was getting exhausted and tired, and as he was leaning into the wind, he suddenly fell over. He sank into the snow and although he hadn't hurt himself, he lay in the snow quite still listening to the wind howling over him.

I've had enough, he thought as he lay there, *I can do no more.*

He closed his eyes and just let his body relax, knowing the cold would soon do the job of ending the quest.

He lay there getting colder as snow settled over him. It was almost a comfort to know that the ordeal would be soon over.

He became aware that the snow was slowing down as was the wind. He moved his head slightly and opened his eyes.

Just to the side of him was the hut; he could see it.

New energy pounded through his veins and he pushed his hands under him and pushed up so that he was sat on his now bent legs.

Yes, it was the hut and just a short way away.

He pushed up on one knee and then stood. He was not very steady but turned to the side and made his way to the hut nonetheless.

If he had kept on walking on his current path, he would have passed it in the snowstorm. If he hadn't turned his head as he lay there, he would have frozen to death, and the house would have won.

New energy came to him, he would not give in, he would not be beaten by 'if'.

He reached the door and opened it. He had done it, he thought, as he entered the door expecting to be greeted by the boys, but no, he was in a hut just like the one he had left.

Or was it the same one? He eased the scratched goggles from his face and put them on the table, then his gloves and then opened his big coat. He needed to get out of the Penguin poo coat.

Scott came to realise that the room was warm, and so he went to unfasten the snow shoes from his coat but they were not there.

He removed the coat and muttered "What the heck," as he saw the coat was now as good as new. The poo was gone!

Scott picked up the goggles to look at his reflection, and could see no poo on his face.

"A shower without getting wet—brilliant!"

The house was undressing him and changing his clothes also. As he looked at the coat put on the chair by Scott, he also noticed that the sun goggles were as new. He had not realised this when he had looked at his reflection just a moment ago.

He looked down at the trousers and they were the same, everything had been put back to as it was when he left the other hut.

He turned to walk over to the window and noticed that, as he walked, so his boots made a tap-tap noise.

His boots had changed. By bending and lifting his foot across his other foot, he could see studs and on the toe cap were points sticking out like little triangle knives. *The house has changed my boots and I never felt a thing*, said Scott to himself.

He looked on the wall for the snowshoes, if the house had taken them, then it might have hung them back up.

No, instead what looked like a mini pickaxe was hanging on the wall. It was pointed at one end and wide at the other

What else had changed? He touched the bear amulet that was still there.

He went to the window and looked out.

He couldn't see much, the snow had stopped but everything just looked white. He stood to the side of the window and tried to see if the door he needed to get back, was in the distance, but no, it was impossible to see.

He looked at the pictures on the wall.

The penguins were pecking him and Scott was just lying there in red ice.

The house was definitely evil. He didn't look at the bear picture—the house was trying to get him even more scared than he was.

He had to move on if he was going to complete this quest.

Scott picked up the goggles and put them on, then lifted them onto the top of his head. Next, he pulled on the coat, and before pulling the hood over the top of his head, adjusted the goggles. He checked to see that his coat was fastened and picked his gloves up.

He walked to the door but then hesitated. He went to the wall and pulled the pickaxe away from the wall.

It had a loop on the end but if it was slung over an arm and someone's head, it could dig into them, Scott thought.

He looked around again and on the table was a belt.

That wasn't there before, said Scott to himself. He returned to the table and picked up the belt; it had a press and click buckle, and also had a small loop for the pickaxe to drop the handle through. This was at the side of any one wearing it, so the blades on the axe would be pointing where he had been and where he was going.

Much safer. If a penguin attacked him on this occasion, then he should be safe if he fell.

Scott dropped the axe into the loop after he had put the belt on.

No adjustment was necessary, the house had made it to fit! Had he forgotten anything?

He decided that he had not and opened the door, slowly checking to see if the bear was outside. He knew the house would be bringing one or more up against him in this quest, but when?

He stepped out and looked around.

It was as if the hut had moved while he was inside. Nothing was the same!

In front of him was a great expanse of ice with ice cliffs in the distance.

Everything was dusted with a light snow covering and it was all very white. As Scott looked around, he was glad he had his goggles on, for he had lifted them slightly when he first stepped out of the hut. The reflected light from the sun above had made his eyes hurt. The goggles would be staying on.

Scott turned to go around the hut but stood still in amazement. The hut was gone. In its place was a post with a sign on it. It had a picture of a hut on it pointing towards the ice cliff.

Scott turned again and started walking. He was able to walk quite well on the ice; his new boots gripped the snowy ice very well.

He was slowly moving upwards. Where the ice had broken, and had been pushed against itself, it created a step. Scott was taking some of these steps to get to the ice cliff face but he couldn't see a hut in front of him.

Scott kept an eye open for the bear or any animal that could be a problem.

As he neared the ice cliff, he could see another sign like the one he found outside the hut.

At last, still climbing up the ice steps, he came to the sign.

This time it showed a hut but it pointed up the ice cliff.

"This is going to be a hard stage," said Scott. He looked around, looking for anything that might help; a ladder or something to help.

On one part of the ice face, he noticed a slight ridge that seemed to be moving upward.

He made his way towards the ridge and unhooked the pickaxe.

Scott looked at the two pick edges, then tried to make a small toe hole in the ice. This seemed to work. He hit the pointed edge into the ice and hung on it. It worked.

He reached up and found a small ridge above the wider one he would use to stand on.

Scott stepped on the wider ridge and pushed the axe into the ice face, further up and away from where he stood.

Using the axe as support, he moved sideways and started to go upwards.

He continued on up, always holding on with his hand as he pulled the axe out and stuck it in the ice face further on. It was a slow and hard climb but Scott soon found a rhythm and made steady progress.

Scott was quite scared about this part of the quest, but as with all of the other rooms, it was 'do it or stay forever'.

He had no choice, so he tried to control his fear.

The ridge ran out.

Scott looked up and could see another ridge above him going back the other way but climbing.

He looked back and saw that if he went back down a short way, another thin shelf intersected the ridge he was on and also the one he needed to be on to get higher

This shelf was quite steep and he would need to be careful, as it was a very narrow ridge.

How to get to it was the next problem.

He tried kicking his spiked toes into the ice but when he put weight on it, his feet slipped out of the hole he had made.

He decided to try again in the same foot hole but to keep kicking to make it deeper—not an easy task whilst hanging on to an ice cliff.

Ice flicked out of the hole and, holding on to the ice pick he thrust his foot into the ice hole and stepped up.

It worked! Taking the pickaxe out of the higher position he had it in, he hit the pick into a higher place and with one toe in his new hole he started to kick a hole higher up using the pickaxe as support.

He soon had his next hole and again stepped up. He was making a ladder in the ice, or like the climbing notches in the other room.

At last he was able to pull himself up onto the new shelf ridge and make his way higher up. Scott didn't want to look down, he knew he shouldn't but as soon as he thought it, he did it.

It was a long way down and Scott clung to the pickaxe as he started to get a bit giddy and feel sick.

He turned to the ice face, gritted his teeth and swallowed hard.

He was not going to lose now. He calmed down and then looking up started moving up on this shelf that was slightly wider than the first one.

Again he got into a rhythm and soon he was able to stand on the top of the ice cliff, but away from the edge.

Scott looked into the distance and could see the penguins still making their way back and forth.

Scott turned around and looked for the route he should take next.

In front of him was another post with a sign on it.

Scott walked up to it and saw that it was pointing away from the cliff's edge.

He started on his way and although it seemed downhill, he was surprised to find that after a very short walk, he had come to a chasm.

He could see the hut on the other side.

He looked down and then across to where the hut was.

I hope I don't have to climb down then up the other side to get to the hut, thought Scott.

He moved towards the edge and then looked both ways to see if a walking ridge was available.

It was at this point that he noticed the rope bridge further along the edge.

Scott walked along towards it, keeping away from   the   edge.
When he got there he almost broke down and cried. The bridge was broken.

Only one side was still in place. The main rope across the gap and the supporting rope with the slats of wood that would have been the walkway still crossed the divide but the other side was gone.

Scott tested the rope by pulling on it, it seemed secure. The posts supporting the ropes were in the ice, and solid.

He looked down at the drop, then decided.

First, he made sure that the axe was safe, then he took hold of the top rope that had been the main hand rope and stepped onto the support rope between the wooden slats still hanging down.

By moving sideways he was able to hold on and step between the wood slats. With each step he was moving downwards with the natural sag in the rope.

As he neared the middle he found that he was leaning out more and more. His weight was causing the imbalance—and it was wobbling.

He gritted his teeth and went on, and slowly started to rise back up from the sag in the rope and, with aching arms and legs, he was across.

He turned and walked back towards the hut, this must be the end now, surely!

He reached the hut and opened the door.

No, it wasn't over yet!

The door shut behind him and he moved to the chair and sat down. He was still in a hut.

Scott looked around, then down to his clothes.

He was still in his white coat and trousers but the shoes were now snow boots, as he had on for the first part of this room.

The snow axe was gone as was the belt.

Amazingly, Scott also noticed that his aches had gone and he did not feel tired. Around his neck was the bear amulet. Nothing else from the other two parts of this room he had done was evident. The pictures on the wall were the same. The Penguins were still marching as the Scott in the picture, having been attacked, lay in a pool of blood. Scott shivered, it was the wish of the house but had not happened. He refused to look at the bear picture, he could see it in the picture but it was not moving as he was not near it. It was just a picture at the moment.

Scott moved to the window. He could see the rope bridge in the distance.

He turned and went to the door, if it was as cold out there as when he came in, the gear he was wearing would give very good protection for him against the cold.

He opened the door and nearly fell over with surprise. The hut was on a mini flat iceberg or floe, and lots of others were all around.

Away in the distance, movement caught his eye. A bear!

He went to turn back into the hut but it wasn't there! Then he saw it appear in the distance on a long flat shelf with an ice wall behind it.

All this took a moment as Scott looked back at the bear.

It was on its way, jumping from one ice floe to another.

Scott moved to the edge of the one he was on and jumped to another that would take him nearer to the hut.

By jumping onto one then moving sideways to another, he could make his way to the firm ground the hut was on.

He glanced to the side from where the bear was coming.

He couldn't see it at first but then saw it swimming towards the next ice floe nearest to it, and it was getting nearer!

Scott took a running jump onto an ice floe, then trying to maintain a line to the hut, he changed direction just after he landed on it and ran towards another reasonable sized floe.

It was a small piece of ice that brought about his downfall.

As Scott turned, he didn't look down, his eyes on his goal, that being the hut.

He was moving fast when his toe hit the ice block and he tripped over onto his stomach and with the momentum, started to slide towards the edge on his belly, just as the Penguins had.

He had to stop—the water's edge was rushing towards him.

He dug his toes into the ice and started to slow down.

Just at the edge, he stopped but his hands were in the water, and as the gloves got wetter, so his hands got colder.

Scott stood and as he did so, the ice floe tipped towards the water.

Scott stepped back and saved himself from falling in the ice cold water.

He took a few steps back and then ran for the next ice floe.

His hands were hurting and he was aware that it was the wet that was coming through the gloves and effecting his hands that was causing the pain.

He ran at the next floe and landed but slowed down before veering towards the next one he needed.

As he jumped on to the next floe, he caught sight of the bear swimming towards the ice floe he was going for—it was trying to cut him off!

He jumped onto the floe—quite a large one—and started running towards the edge.

He was close to the solid ice and the ice floe he was on was going to get him nearer to the solid ice edge the hut was on.

He reached the edge of the floe he was on and jumped onto a small ice floe then stopped to see what one to go for, then making his decision he turned sideways and ran to the edge.

Just as he ran and went to jump, the ice floe lifted him high up in the air just like a see-saw. He flew into the air, much higher than he wanted.

The bear had landed onto the ice floe that Scott had been running on and it's weight had tilted the floe upwards just as he had ran and jumped.

Scott went very high and as he descended, missed the floe he was going for, but as luck would have it the waves caused by the bear jumping on the floe, seemed to make the flat ice floes bump and knock together. Another ice floe's edge moved into the gap that Scott was likely to fall into.

He landed on the edge, gained his balance and then ran to the other side and just jumped onto the next ice floe. No planning now, it was just get to the hut.

He felt the floe he was on start to rock, but didn't look. He knew what was behind him.

He jumped onto a small floe then straight in front of him onto another bigger one.

Pausing for just a moment to get his route in mind he jumped onto the next small floe.

He ran to the edge and jumped onto another bigger one but then felt the floe he was on rise, as the bear landed just behind him.

The roar behind him caused his limbs to stop working as fear went through his body. He had lost.

Then he remembered the amulet!

Scott pulled open the coat, his fingers not working very well with the pain, and took hold of the amulet.

He threw it at the bear and as it landed at its feet, a part-eaten seal appeared. Blood was all over the ice.

Without waiting, Scott turned and ran towards the next ice floe he needed, and jumped. He heard the bear roar again but not quite as close as it was when his legs froze in fright.

He kept up the running and jumping on the floes and finally landed onto the solid ice. He glanced back then slowed down, the bear was eating the rest of the seal, its fur red around its face from its meal.

Scott jogged to the hut and pulled a glove from his hand.

His fingers and his hand were black and really painful.

This was called frostbite but he didn't know this, it just hurt and panicked him that it was so black. He did his best to grip the door handle and opened it.

He stepped into a hut. His heart sank.

Still he had not finished the quest.

This hut had a door at the other end and this hut was longer.

Scott felt the pain in his fingers and hand easing and then, when he was halfway to the other door, he appeared to be back to normal. His hands had returned to the normal colour and the pain was gone.

He walked to the end of the hut and noticed the red stone in front of the door.

He stepped onto the red stone, reached out to the door handle and opened it.

He walked back into the house.

The boys ran up to him and questions came pouring out to Scott. "Tell us about the room Scott," asked Two.

"Was it witches and broomsticks?" asked Three.

Scott sat on the stairs and again told the story of the room as the room's door painted itself white with a penguin and a bear on it.

"The room that I went into this time was an ice room," said Scott.

"I went there," said Two.

"WE KNOW," shouted the two other boys. "Let Scott tell us about it." Scott told them about the clothes just appearing on him, the snow shoes and then the penguins.

"What are penguins?" asked One.

"He must be old," said Two. "They are birds that don't fly," said Two.

"They swim under water," said Three.

"Swim under water, birds fly, not swim," said One. "I think you are fooling around with me."

"Never mind for now," said Scott, "they attacked me and pecked me all over my body and squirted poo over me."

"Ugh, thank goodness you become clean once you come out of the room."

"I can only agree with that," said Scott and then told the boys about the broken bridge and lastly, the bear.

"I wonder if it ate me," said Two.

The boys looked at Two, then turned to Scott. "So nine quests completed," said One.

"Just one to go," said Three. "You have done so well Scott.

They all looked at Scott and then moved back down to the hall. They wanted him to start the last quest, but didn't want to say it.

Scott stood up and moved downstairs.

He looked at each of the boys and then, without saying anything, moved to the next door.

Chapter 12
The Tenth and Final Quest

He took the door's handle, pressed it down and opened the door. He was aware that he might never see the three boys ever again or become part of this house.

It all depended on this last quest; it was all down to him. He stepped into the room.

Scott looked down at the red stone as he stepped sideways. He then looked up into the room. He was on the last stage of the quest and didn't want to fail now.

In front of him was a huge vista of high mountains, rocky valleys and green plains with rivers running through them.

"Well, house," said Scott, "you really have created a lovely room now. I can't see the beginning or any end as I stand here looking around." He turned around to check the door but it was gone.

In its place were even more views of the countryside. It was spectacular. Mountains reached up to the sky, small amounts of snow still remained on the peaks. Birds were singing and Scott thought how beautiful it all was.

What was he to do? The red stone he was standing on was the only thing out of place in this wonderful land created by the house, and it was created, he reminded himself as he turned back to the view he had first looked on.

In front of him was a small rocky path dropping down to the valley below. Rocks that had fallen from the mountain lay strewn along the way, and scrub bushes had grown over it, softening the view. Further down the valley, trees grew. It was a room, but it was more like another world.

The red stone gave a shake and Scott turned, trying to maintain his position on the stone. The stone had reduced to half its size.

I guess the house wants me to get on with it, he said to himself.

Scott could not see the exit door but as there was only one path, he assumed that this was the way to start.

Just as he was going to step down to the path, a roar came from behind him and then a strong gust of wind passed him. A huge, red dragon flew overhead and landed on a high rock in the valley below him.

"What the heck!" said Scott. He stood back up from the crouched position on the red stone, for he had ducked down at the noise and the wind from the Dragon's massive wings as it flew over him. "Now what," he said aloud. "How am I going to get past that?"

The red stone gave another shake but did not reduce in size any more.

Scott looked behind him to see if he could take a different route away from the dragon, but below him on this side was a rocky slope with areas that he would need to climb down, and with a flying dragon who had no need to climb, it was a big no-no!

As he started to turn around again, he noticed a stone with a lot of script on it. It was not in the English language but maybe it would be in English on another side.

He had to move, and the dragon was looking the other way. He stepped down and ran down the slope to the stone, pleased that as he reached it, the dragon was lost to his view. *If I can't see it, then maybe it can't see me*, he thought.

He looked at the script but could not read it. "This is no good to me, what I need is a translation," he said out loud, and as his last word was spoken, so the stone writing changed, and became an English translation.

The house had listened! This is what he read:

On your quest you've done quite well,
More than expected, truth to tell
In this quest three guardians fly
Here to stop you as you try.
Should you burn, turn to dust,
In the house, stay you must.
A spire will stand for three domains
Where my guardians live and reign
Find three amulets made for me,
Then from this quest you'll be free.

Scott reread the rhyme and thought about three guardians that could fly.

As he thought about this, fear came into his heart; this must be the biggest challenge yet. "Three Dragons," exclaimed Scott out loud. "I need George the Dragon Slayer to help me on this quest!"

He sneaked a look around the rock—the dragon had gone.

So far, so good, he said to himself.

A blob of red-coloured jelly fell from above him, and as he looked up, he made eye contact with the dragon who was sitting on the rock he had been reading the message from.

Scott turned and ran into the trees behind the rock and then dropped down to crawl under a rock that had fallen and was rested on another, at an angle. His heart was beating very fast, that had been scary.

He heard a noise, like something dragging along, and turned in his confined space to look out to where he had come from.

The dragon was on the floor pushing small rocks out of the way and flattening the scrub.

It gave a snort and then let out a long roar as it blew out a fiery jet, burning the scrub in front of the fallen stone Scott was hiding under.

Scott felt the heat and was having trouble breathing with the smoke.

I have got to get out of here, he thought, *but how?*

He looked around and saw that the stone he was under was leaning against another, and if he could squeeze around the corner without the dragon seeing him, he might be able to get away.

He got on his belly and crawled along to the back of the stone he was under then turned and pushed his feet through the gap between the two fallen boulders.

It was a tight fit but Scott found that if he kept his arms up, he could push himself into the gap and by turning this way and that, get into the gap. With a final push he succeeded and was able to manoeuvre beneath this rock.

As he looked for his next route out and away from the dragon, a great gush of fiery breath came into the space he had just left.

If he had stayed he would now be toast!

If anything could be funny about his present situation, it was that the fire-breath was red, just like the dragon! It made Scott smirk as he thought it, but he must move on.

He advanced to the end of the rock he was under, and looked out from the cover he had. He first looked upwards—no Dragon there! Then he looked at the route in front of him. It was a gentle slope going down to the valley and he was against the mountain's edge. He could see parts sticking out and lots of loose stone resting against the mountain's side. He thought it was called 'screed' although why he wanted to waste time thinking about correct words, he was not sure.

He needed to calm down, he was sure this was his nerves causing his mind to think silly thoughts when he should be concentrating on getting away from there.

He saw that the best route for him was under the thick scrub, away from the rocks—the scrub had grown thicker there and would cover his movement as he moved further down into the valley, and to where trees grew as the valley dropped.

Scott ducked down and in a crouching run, zigzagged under each bush keeping a general route towards the next mega pile of stones from the mountain.

He got to the edge of the scrub and looked for a gap between the rocks that he had seen as he made his way down.

By moving towards the mountain's edge, he saw how a huge slab had come down and rested on another, at an angle and was giving him the gap he wanted.

He came out into the clear and ran to the gap. Behind him a screech came and a mighty rush of wind.

He ducked into the gap and crawled along as far as he could.

Another gap in front allowed him to proceed at an angle away from the one he had been in. It wasn't much room but by wriggling he was able to crawl into a bigger gap under a huge boulder. This was not totally covered and a small tree was growing up through the gap, covering the hole slightly. As Scott crawled past the tree trunk, it shook and then a snort by the red dragon above put more haste into Scott's legs as he squeezed past it. The dragon breathed out and burnt the top of the tree leaving the trunk burning under the stone where Scott was.

Panic hit Scott and he crawled along the small gap into the next gap under the fallen stones.

He looked back and saw the dragon's long fingers and talons poking down through the gap.

It's trying to winkle me out, he said to himself.

He had been breathing fast as he rested under this safe gap, but he knew he had to move on.

He looked around for his next move but found none!

He was trapped.

The dragon blew another fiery breath into the gap and Scott watched the tree become charcoal and go out as it fell to the floor in smouldering ash. Scott shuddered as he thought, *this could have been me*. What a way to go!

As the dragon climbed onto the rock, daylight went as it blocked out the small amount of light that was coming from the gap.

Scott looked around, then saw a small gap with light showing through at the back of the rock he was under.

He picked up a flat rock and using it to scrape away the soil, he started to expand the hole.

It meant that he would need to wriggle under the big rock but he could now see that there was a big gap beyond the space he was in.

With more effort he cleared a big gap and once he felt he had enough cleared, he pushed his head in and looked into the space.

Hooray! It was a large space and it looked as if he might have quite a few exits to choose from.

Scott pulled himself through the hole and looked around.

A giant boulder was holding up quite a few other huge rocks that formed the roof of the cave he was in. Four clear exits were easy to see from the giant boulder, as he moved around it plus the hole that he had come through.

He needed to make sure that the route he picked would take him on down in to the valley where he felt he should be able to start his search for the amulet for the red dragon.

He had not seen a spire as he had looked around from the red stone but with nothing to go on. He had to start somewhere.

The slope of the ground gave him the best idea, so he moved to the nearest hole and eased himself through.

It was rather like a corridor for a short way, then he had to climb down the broken rock fragments not unlike steps. Still under larger rocks and great slabs of Flint laying across them acting like a roof, he continued on down.

Sometimes he had to get on his stomach and crawl commando style to maintain his descent safely.

He started to run out of cover but he was very near the valley's lowest point. Staying still for a moment he listened to the sounds around him. Trees had replaced most of the scrub bushes in front of him.

Birds sang and he could hear water bubbling along somewhere just a little lower.

He picked the nearest bank of trees, all bigger than the scrub he had left further up the valley, and pulled out of the cover and ran to the trees.

Once under them, he went around the trunk and looked back up the way he had come.

The dragon was sitting on a rock up the valley, looking down at the rocks near where the tree had been. A small plume of black smoke still drifted up from the hole.

Scott turned and walked towards the river he could hear, but keeping under the dense cover of the trees to stop the red dragon from seeing him.

He broke through the trees and low scrub under the trees and came to the bank.

Scott followed the bank down and as it levelled out, he came to an open space.

In front of him was a triangular spire with red painted on the side facing Scott and green on another. He could not see the other side's colour but was it important to find out now? Clearly, he was at the point of the boundary of the red dragon and of a green dragon.

Logic didn't show its head and Scott decided he wanted to know!

Scott moved over to the spire and looked around to the other side to see the colour. It was blue, but he had made a mistake!

He heard a screech and looked up the valley.

The red dragon was flying down the valley. It had seen him. He wouldn't make it back under the trees in time.

Scott ran around the spire and stood behind it, watching the dragon. It stopped and moved close to the spire that Scott was behind.

It didn't cross the invisible line that divided the three areas.

The red dragon moved away slightly and sank down, watching Scott.

"You missed out on your meal Mr Red Dragon," said Scott as he watched him.

Then it happened, Scott was thrown to the floor by a very strong force, and he felt his body being pressed into the ground as the green dragon gripped him with one of its talons, pressing Scott to the ground.

Scott could not move and could hardly draw breath, as the weight of the dragon pressed down on him.

The red dragon stood up as this happened and advanced towards the green dragon.

Both were snarling at each other and the red dragon suddenly attacked the green dragon.

Talons raked towards the green dragon who let go of Scott and raised its talons towards the red dragon's attack.

Scott pulled himself up and ran to the blue dragon's side of the spire.

He had been knocked between the red dragon and the green dragon's area and this had started the squabble between them. Not stopping, he ran to the safety of the trees on the blue side and sank to the ground. He was hurt; one talon had cut his shoulder and his back where the green dragon had hit him as it grabbed him. All because he was stupid and wanted to find out what the third dragon's colour was!

He was alive but he felt very sick with the shock that he had so very nearly died in this the last room in this quest. He must stay focused!

Now he was in the blue dragon's area.

He picked himself up and limped along under the tree cover, keeping an eye on the two dragons that were still facing each other, but now not fighting.

Scott made his way around in a circle, crossing the invisible boundary back into the red dragon's area. He kept under the trees until he was behind the red dragon, he then turned and walked deeper into the tree cover away from the red dragon.

He had no way of knowing what he was looking for, but standing still would not find it. Scott found the river again and climbed up, this time towards the mountain, following the waters flow.

He reached the point where the water fell as a waterfall into the river.

Scott moved closer, looking for a stone with writing on it or something like this that could indicate a hiding place.

He suddenly had a thought; what if there was a cave behind the waterfall? He moved closer and tried to look through the falls.

It's no good, he thought. *I am going to have to go into the water and under the falls.*

Looking around quickly, he dropped into the water and waded up to the falls, and taking a deep breath, walked under the waterfall.

He found that there was a cave and steps at the side climbing to a flat area.

As he climbed up, he saw that in the middle of the area was what looked like a stone table, and on it, was a small red image of the red dragon.

He picked it up and felt a quiver run through his body. It was just like a mild electric shock.

He nearly dropped it but fortunately didn't.

He had the red dragon's talisman, but what now?

He returned to the falls and waded out once again. He stood still, as shock ran through him—the red dragon was in front of him and its head was about one foot away from him.

He had lost! He closed his eyes, he didn't want to see what was coming.

He stood still waiting for the teeth to crunch him to bits, but nothing happened.

He opened his eyes and looked at the dragon. It was still in front of him, just watching him.

Scott moved back slowly away from it, intending to go back under the falls, but the dragon moved one great arm around Scott and cut his retreat off.

It hooked a talon under Scott's shirt and lifted him up and put him on to the river bank.

Scott sank to the grassy bank, his heart beating faster than ever as he tried to get his breathing under control. It was not going to eat him.

He opened his hand and looked at the talisman of the red dragon.

As he opened his hand, the image glowed. The dragon sank down and watched Scott.

The talisman had tamed the dragon—that was what the shock was that he had felt on picking up the red dragon's talisman. The power had transferred to Scott as he had picked it up.

Scott stood up and walked down the river bank retracing his steps towards the open area with the triangle spire.

Although he was still hurting, he was feeling quite good in knowing that he had one dragon tamed and now had to try to get two more.

He glanced back to the dragon and saw that it was still sitting by the river.

Scott came down to the open area with the spire in it.

The red dragon flew down to where Scott stood and landed close by. It looked at him then sat down.

"I wonder if you are hoping I am going to drop the talisman so it breaks and you can then eat me?" said Scott to it.

Not expecting an answer, Scott walked to the green dragon's area.

The dragon was no longer there, it must have flown away after the fight with the red one.

Scott walked over to the tree line and moved into the cover of the trees. He pushed the talisman into his pocket and then started on his way.

He walked towards the mountain's edge still under the trees, aware that he needed to keep under cover from the green dragon.

He started moving up the green dragon's area and started looking for any sign of an amulet. No big river was falling down this part of the valley, just a little stream, so it wasn't behind another waterfall.

Scott had not been aware that the trees he was under, were giving less and less cover as he moved up the valley. He heard a roar and then talons swept past him as he dropped to the ground.

As the green dragon rose and turned to strike again, Scott ran to the rocks at the mountain-side and ducked under a rock slab.

He quickly crawled into the hole and around a bend made by yet another rock that had landed at an angle.

He looked around the corner and saw a huge eye at the entrance that he had crawled in.

The green dragon was looking for him, and as it had almost caught him before, it was very keen to do so again.

Scott ducked back around the corner, away from the eye, and looked for another gap he might crawl through.

Smaller rocks had fallen at the end of the cover he was under but there was no sign of a way out.

He heard a snort and then a great tongue of fire shot down the gap that Scott had escaped through. He pushed himself close to the corner rock as the flame's force hit the end of the first gap and bent around the second tunnel that Scott was in.

Scott saw the rocks start to fall as yet another burst of fire followed the first.

Scott was very hot but the flames had passed him as he pressed against the tight angle of the second rock.

And then the flame just stopped.

Scott stayed still not daring to move in case he made a noise.

The grass that had grown through the gaps in the small rocks at the end of the gap was burning, the smoke from which was making it difficult to breath. Scott wanted to cough. The more he thought about it, the more he needed to cough.

Then he heard a snort at the entrance and he knew the dragon was not gone.

He moved very slowly towards the smouldering grass and as he did so, he felt the ground tremor and start to give way.

Scott fell through a hole beneath his feet and small rocks followed him down.

Then the big flat rock that had formed the roof of the rock tunnel he was in, fell on top of the hole, trapping him inside the hole he had fallen through.

As the dust settled, Scott found that he could see around him as light seemed to be filtering through gaps along the cave's side that he was now in.

Standing still, making sure that his eyes became accustomed to the light, he then slowly made his way towards the best source of light.

Layers of flat stones had fallen onto the big boulder and formed a roof but not totally covered all of the roof space above.

This was clearly a risky part, as the dragon could see him and burn him as he passed by.

He moved away from this part that was giving light, and made his way to the next source of light.

This was coming from a possible tunnel a bit higher up. Scott decided to climb up and explore this as a possible escape route from his foe.

He could hear the dragon snorting outside but he thought it was a little further away from where he was now.

He climbed up the mud and shingle slope, and looked into the tunnel, for that was what it was. He crawled into it and made his way, on hands and knees, towards the light.

At the end of the tunnel he stopped. No turns had been available as he had crawled but as he looked out, he could see the dragon further down near where Scott had run into the first rock tunnel.

He was higher now.

He looked up the valley and noticed an old house that was just about standing but had no roof on it. It was open ground going up with loose screed that would make a noise as he walked on it.

Bet the dragon ate the owner, thought Scott.

He looked down at the dragon and decided to climb up the stones towards the old house. No cover would help him here, it was a question of moving quietly and hoping the dragon would not see him.

Once the dragon heard him he would run and hope.

Scott moved out and picking the least amount of loose stone in front of him, started his way up.

He could see more boulders behind the broken building—this must have been the cause of the damage to the house.

He had made it halfway when he slipped and fell, causing a minor avalanche of loose stone screed to move on down. He picked himself up quickly and ran towards the house as he knew the dragon was on its way by the mighty roar it gave behind him.

Scott scrambled up and got to the house just as a long jet of fire came towards him.

As he turned around the stone wall of the house the flame caught up with him and hit his trousers. He was on fire.

He dived under a huge rock leaning against the wall of the house and tripped on a stone jutting up at an angle.

He fell over and tumbled onto his bottom, and found himself sliding down on a flat rock deeper into the ground.

He came to a halt as a pile of stones, dust and dirt followed him down.

After a few moments, he felt the pain on his bottom from the fire. He quickly stood, banging his head on the sloping stone above, and brushed his trousers on his bottom.

The fire was out, thanks to the dust and the slide down the stone slope as he dropped down to his new hole in the ground.

Scott felt around, but gently, as he was feeling sore and he knew he had been burnt.

A large hole was in the back of his trousers and his pants were the only thing covering his bum!

"What am I going to say to Mum when I get home," he said aloud. "She's going to kill me."

Then he started to laugh as what he had said suddenly came to him. The dragon was trying to do that very thing!

He was in shock after such a close encounter with the dragon.

His head hurt, his bottom was sore from the burn, his arm was bleeding where he had fallen and his toe hurt where he had tripped. His back hurt from the green dragon squashing him when it had attacked him earlier and had dug its talons into him. No doubt about it, he was an aching mess.

Why don't I just give up? he thought, but as the thought came he slowly stood up and looked around his cave.

No way, he thought, *I have got this far, I will never give in.*

He eased himself along the stone and the house wall.

I must be next to the cellar of the house, he thought, *as I am below ground.*

He came to the corner of the house and had to climb over a large boulder, then squeeze through a small hole to get to the back of the house.

A large hole was in the back of the house, and he made his way through. Inside, he saw steps going down and decided he should go down.

Very little light was available to show him his way, and he almost stopped.

Now, in front of him, he could make out a glow.

As he came to the bottom of the stairs, he turned a corner and came into the room.

He had an idea that this must have been a wine cellar, an annex of the one above him.

In front of him, on a stone pedestal, was the second dragon talisman for the dragon outside.

He reached up and took hold of the talisman and felt the slight electric shock run through him. The green dragon was his.

He turned and, holding it in his hand, made his way back up the stairs. He was now back in the cellar. He moved across the room and started to climb the next set of stairs into the ground floor of the house.

He paused and looked for the green dragon. He was taking no chances now.

The dragon was sitting on a rock high above him, and as he came out of the front of the house, it just turned its head and looked at Scott.

Scott felt in his pocket for the other talisman, he had forgotten about it and could have lost it. It was still there, but now with two, he would need to think of something he could use to carry them.

Holding the new talisman, Scott started on his way back down to the valley. It was so much easier now as he could follow the rough path to and from the house, and he didn't need to hide from the green dragon.

He looked behind him but the dragon was in the same place, sitting on the rock and watching Scott move on down to the valley.

Scott was limping slightly. He was cut and bruised and there were aches in about all of his body, and then there was the burnt trousers and his scorched football pants showing through the trousers.

He felt exhausted.

At last he came to the open plain where the spire stood.

The green dragon was sitting on the grass in its area alongside the red dragon.

Scott had not seen the dragon fly over him to land on the grass in the open plain.

He was not paying attention to his surroundings, and this could be dangerous.

He lay on the grass for a while and rested. How was he going to keep the talisman he had for both dragons safe? He had no bag. If he put them somewhere, would the house move them to some other place? *They will need to be with me*, he decided, *then I can control the dragons.*

Then he had an idea, if I take my pants off, I may be able to tie the talisman into it and carry it.

He dropped his trousers then his pants, then quickly pulled his trousers back on. He was a little embarrassed about what he was doing.

He looked at his pants with footballs all over it, his favourite pair. The green dragon had scorched them at the back, then he became aware of a chill on his bottom. He had no back on them and his bottom was on show. He decided to rethink the idea.

Scott took off his trousers again and pulled his pants back on. Another idea came. If, by tying a knot in one leg of his trousers he could make a big pocket, he could carry both talismans safely. He made sure that the end was tied tight, then dropped both of the talismans into the leg.

Good, now he had a big pocket, but how to carry it and leave his hands free?

He thought about tying the other leg around himself but that didn't work when he tried. Then he looked at the hole at the crutch and the back of his trousers. If he put his head through that, then he would be able to put his hand down the other leg and he would be wearing it as a big pocket or some sort of weird bag.

He pushed his head through the burnt hole and with a small rip, his head went through.

He slipped his hand up the spare leg and folded the end over, like a cuff, as it was a little too long, but it worked quite well.

He glanced at the two dragons and turned to the last area to finish the quest.

Still feeling battered and bruised, he started towards the trees and then, once under cover, turned and made his way into the last dragon's domain.

He was under the trees but the ground was going downwards and he was beginning to see that the cover was getting less and less as he descended. The river that he had followed on the red dragon's part of the valley was running through this third of the valley. The water was getting closer to his side as he continued to descend and cover was now very poor as the trees had very little soil to support them.

Scott looked at the route in front of him and realised that he would need to cross the river.

Well, he was wearing his pants as if it was a swimming costume he was wearing, he thought, so he was going to get wet.

Where was the dragon on this side hiding? It must be aware that he was here somewhere, did the dragons communicate with each other or was it the house?

Looking around, still under cover, Scott decided to slightly back track on himself and cross further up. Cover would be greater there and he might even get branches over lapping both of the sides, he could only hope!

He retraced his steps and after a short way, found what he wanted.

He stepped down the river bank and keeping an eye on the sky he could see through the cover he waded in.

It was quite deep and quite wide, wider than he had expected.

He had got halfway across, still looking up, when a spout of fire hit his arm, and the trouser leg he was wearing on his arm caught fire.

He screamed and fell into the water putting the fire out as he saw the blue dragon walking down the river under the trees he had been under, a few moments ago.

Scott was on his back midstream floating away from the dragon, and he pushed his feet down and on finding ground thrust himself away from the dragon even more.

The water took him faster as he got midstream and he turned and swam as fast as he could away from the advancing dragon.

The dragon must have realised that his prey was getting away, for it stopped and again blew out a stream of fire at Scott.

Luckily, Scott was moving very fast now and he was soaked, so when the fiery breath hit him, only steam came.

Scott continued to swim not looking back, in truth, it was just blind panic that was causing him to swim so fast.

He was going very fast now and he became aware that it was not his swimming that was getting him away so quickly, it was something else. Then he knew what it was—he could hear it.

He started to try to swim to the opposite side but the current was far too strong. He was going to go over a waterfall.

He held on to his trousers and prepared himself for whatever was going to happen once he went over the falls.

To a thunderous roar both from the falls and an angry dragon, Scott went over the top.

As he fell, he took a deep breath and curled up as if he had jumped in a swimming pool to 'bomb' his mates.

A rush of wings as he fell reminded him that the dragon wanted him and talons just missed him as he fell.

It seemed a long time before he hit the water, yet it was most likely only a short while, but as Scott hit the water with his bottom first, he yelled out and swallowed water as the pain on his burnt bottom took the full impact.

Scott went straight down, no air in his lungs, then rose with the rush of the river as it pushed him away from the falls.

Like a cork, Scott bobbed up and coughed up water as he gasped for air.

He was now under an overhang of trees and as he became more aware of his situation, he also became aware that the water was widening and becoming shallow again. Also, the cover was very much less.

Scott stood and rushed to the opposite bank that he had been trying to get to before he encountered the blue dragon.

He pulled himself up and rushed under the thick tree covering as the blue dragon flew down and landed in the shallow water.

Scott ran deeper into the trees then quickly turned to go back up towards the waterfall.

It was just in time as the trees he had ran under burst into flames as the dragon breathed fire in both directions in a fit of frustrated anger.

Scott kept going, making his way upwards. He had an idea where to look for the last talisman and he wasn't going to stop.

The dragon would have no idea which way he had gone unless it saw him, so Scott took extra care to remain under cover.

His arm hurt where the trouser leg had been burnt, and he decided to stop and check the amulets were still in the trousers.

He looked at the trouser leg that had got the full force of the flame—very little was left. The bottom part hung down like a bit of rag, but he still had his head through the part where his bottom should be.

The amulets were safe.

"My mother's going to ground me when she sees me next time, looking like this," he said out loud.

Even part of his hair was singed.

He pulled the trousers over his head again and tied the half of this trouser leg around the top of his arm, he didn't want that snagging on a thorn or something if he was running from the dragon.

Scott made steady progress up the valley, stopping and keeping still every time he heard the dragon fly above the tree line.

It was searching for him, but Scott thought by keeping quiet, he would not be helping it.

The roar of the waterfall was now getting very loud and the trees were getting less as more stone and rocks became the main thing in front of the waterfall.

Scott knew he could not wade in the water and as it was an open area with just rocks, he would need an idea how to advance further.

The Dragon flew past the tree edge Scott was under, then crossed the waterfall, and having turned, flew back down the river, away from Scott.

Without thinking about it, Scott rushed from cover and ran over the screed and small stones and boulders and reached the large boulders that would give him cover.

He ducked under a huge slab that was leaning against the side of the rock face to the side of the waterfall. Following the gap he climbed over the next small boulder and dropped behind another boulder.

He was safe for the moment.

He was not sure if the Dragon had seen him but he had reasoned that if its back was to him as it flew down river, then he had a chance, and so he had taken it.

It might not know he was under these rocks.

Scott moved along the side of the cliff face under the rocks and came to the water's edge.

Could the last amulet also be under the waterfall?

He could see under the waterfall as he stood to the side and sure enough, his idea looked even more likely. He could see a cave's platform halfway up under the waterfall, but how could he get up there? The drop was quite high, and Scott had fallen from it!

He looked around and found that the sloping boulder he was under, had an even bigger slab resting over the one he was under.

He reasoned that if he could climb above the slab he now was under, he could then move closer to the platform he could see. He decided to go back and try to climb to the higher rock.

Keeping under cover as best as he could, he retraced his steps then climbed up onto the higher rock. He again moved along the rock, moving higher as it was leaning against the rock face. He was no longer under cover, but by using the slope of the rock, he was gaining height. At its maximum height, the rock levelled out. Another flat rock, leaning against the side, with a gap beneath it, gave him a small chance of cover and he ducked under it.

At last he could see that he was almost near enough to get on to the platform. He would need to climb near the edge of the waterfall, from his safe hiding place, again in the open.

He watched for the dragon to fly past the falling water and then stepped out onto the rock and moving sideways went almost under the waterfall. He then climbed up and after a short time reached the cave's platform.

He walked into the cave and came to a passage that split, one going up and one going down.

Which way?

He decided to go up.

He started to go up the passageway and after a short way, it turned upon itself as it rose, and then reversed again to the way it had started.

Scott trudged on, very tired and sore. He again came to another turning.

This again reversed its route after a while and was still going up. It was an upward zigzag.

Scott continued his way up and then saw daylight.

He came to yet another corner but now it turned a new way, and Scott could see the end of the tunnel.

He could also hear the river and the roar of the waterfall.

He came to the end of the tunnel but stopped before going out.

In front of him was a big flat rock by the side of the river and on the flat rock was a huge pile of sticks and branches of trees. Could it be the dragon's nest?

Do they have nests?

This was mythical creatures, so who knows!

Not so mythical now!

These thoughts and more ran through Scott's mind as he looked at the flat rock and the 'nest,' if it was that.

As he looked at this, his hand had gone into his trousers and he was handling the other talisman he had.

The nest glowed under the pile of sticks and Scott could make out the shape of the last talisman he needed. It was on the edge of the nest on the flat rock.

It had responded to the other two he had touched as he puzzled what to do.

Scott stepped out and looked around. No sign of the dragon.

He looked around the corner and saw it was coming along the treetops towards him.

He ducked back inside the tunnel and waited. When he thought the dragon would be on its way back, he stepped out and looked back along the edge of the waterfall and along the treetops below.

The dragon was flying back again on its circuitous route so Scott ran to the flat stone.

He reached in under the pile of sticks, but couldn't find it. Then he remembered to hold the other talismans. He pushed his hand into the trouser pocket and clutched the two and sure enough the blue one glowed, but he was in the wrong place.

He withdrew his hand and as he did, glanced back. The blue dragon was on his way to him.

Scott ran to the side a little further along and thrust his hand into the pile of sticks and touched the amulet.

The dragon came on but then flew over Scott, as Scott felt the now familiar electrical shock.

He had done it.

He pulled out the blue amulet and sank to the floor. Letting his heart settle down, he was surprised to find he was crying.

Shock, fear, or relief—he wasn't sure but he had completed the quest.

Now he had to find the door.

He looked at the blue dragon and then got up and started to walk away from the waterfall.

As he started, he became aware that the dragon was behind him and as he turned, the dragon clamped both its claws around a flat stone and moved towards Scott.

Scott stood still, he had no fight left in him.

The dragon lifted its head over Scott and just as Scott thought it was going to bite his head off, it nudged him towards his feet where the stone was.

Scott was pushed towards the stone again and his legs hit the edge of it, causing him to fall on it.

The dragon looked between its legs and saw that Scott was lying on it. As Scott picked himself up, the dragon spread its vast wings.

"It must be going to take me back to the spire," he said to himself.

Scott turned and sat on the stone and held onto the dragon's talons on each side.

The Blue Dragon lifted up its legs as he started to fly, with Scott on a stone between its legs.

He watched the river below him rush by, holding on to the Dragon as he went.

In a very short time, the dragon reached the spire and circled it. It then started to fly with the other two dragons following. It flew up the valley to the door that Scott had come through, and that had now magically reappeared.

The dragons set down next to the door and Scott got off of the dragon's stone and walked to the red stone.

Three shapes, one above the other were now carved into the door and Scott could see it was the same shape as the amulets in his trousers.

He reached in and took one out, it was the green one.

He slotted it in at the top then took the next one out.

It was the red one, he pushed that one into the middle slot and reached for the last one, the blue one.

He slotted it in the last place under the rest and stood to open the door.

No handle appeared.

He stepped back and looked at it, and saw that the blue one at the bottom was glowing in the door.

He changed the order of the amulets in the door, the red at the top, then the green and they all glowed.

He glanced back to look at the Dragons but they had disappeared. A handle appeared and Scott opened the door and walked through.

Behind him, the door closed and painted itself, this time in three triangles with a dragon in each section.

Scott became aware that the trousers he had over his head were no longer there.

He had not felt them disappear but they were gone.

He looked down and found he was wearing them just as he had when he went through the door.

Well, he thought *at least I don't need to give explanations to Mum.*

He was also no longer aching, or burnt. He felt fine. It was an amazing feeling, but totally weird.

The spell was broken and each boy was now in their own clothes.

One was in a strange baggy pair of trousers, the legs of the trousers tucked into his socks. His shirt was very loose with a frill on it and he wore a coat that had a collar that stood up on its own.

"I am Ruffus," said One, "and I thank you for setting me free."

As he moved forward to embrace Scott, he changed into smoke and it floated upwards.

Two was also dressed in his own clothes and as he walked towards Scott, he said, "I am Robert and..." He didn't finish his sentence as he also changed to smoke and drifted upwards.

Three called out that he was George but changed into smoke as he moved towards Scott.

Scott looked at the smoke and then moved to the front door. As he did, the door opened on its own and Scott stepped out.

Jack ran up to Scott and grabbed Scott's hand. "Come on mate, let's get going before any one comes," said Jack with slight panic in his voice.

Scott looked at Jack and laughed and said, "No one's coming out after me, Jack."

"You are joking, mate," said Jack. "When that door slammed, it must have woken whoever is in there, now let's get the heck out of here." He picked up his bike and looked back at the door still open.

"What have you done, Scottie? There is smoke coming out the door now, how much damage have you done in so little time?"

Scott smiled. He touched his head and realised his bicycle helmet was on his head. The house had done it again.

So little time, yet it felt like years to me, he thought as he watched the three boys disappear in three plumes of smoke.

He felt quite sad as he watched the boys in the form of smoke disappear, he never had the chance to get to know them.

"Well, we are all free now and back to our own time," Scott said aloud, as he felt for his mobile phone in his trouser pocket.

It was there, but by now, Scott expected no less of the house.

He got on his bike and cycled slowly up the drive, led by Jack.

They were halfway towards the gates when a loud rumble behind them caused both boys to stop.

The top of the house started to fall in and then the second floor also collapsed into the remains of the building.

"Scotty, I don't know what you did in that house but this is down to you," said Jack. "I'm not taking the blame for this," and he turned and cycled to the gate. Scott watched the house crash down to a pile of rubble—nothing seemed to be left standing. As the dust cleared and settled, a piece of paper floated down in front of Scott. He looked down at it and then picked it up. It was the painting, but was looking up the drive, with four boys, three walking down the drive—one after the other. It wasn't moving now, it was a real painting... The last boy in the picture was Scott on his bike!

Scott looked at it once again, then rolled it up. He had his memories of the four boys who were locked in the house all in the order they had come in to it; the house had provided it for him.

He turned and peddled up the last of the drive and without looking back, put his hand on Jack's shoulder and said, "Come on, Jack, let's go home, I'm hungry."